T0363222

Leon Silver

sweeties

[Lacuna]
2016

Published in 2016 by Lacuna in New South Wales, Australia
http://www.lacunapublishing.com

Lacuna is an imprint of Golden Orb Creative
http://www.goldenorbcreative.com

All enquiries to the publisher: general@lacunapublishing.com

Cover design by Golden Orb Creative
Cover photograph © Rinofelino | Dreamstime.com

Text design and production by Golden Orb Creative
Typeset in 11pt Adobe Caslon Pro

National Library of Australia Cataloguing-in-Publication entry

Silver, Leon, author

Sweeties / Leon Silver

ISBN: 9781922198266 (paperback)

ISBN: 9781922198273 (ebook)

Loss of consciousness--Fiction. Pinball machines--Fiction.
Early memories--Fiction.

A823.4

PULL THE PIN, HEAR THE PING, SILVER BALL BOUNCE AND DING ... Arm over arm, legs kicking, head twisting, breathing in, then out, so ordinary a Monday morning; inconceivable that anything out of the ordinary can happen, as Abel Jackson Marvin does his usual laps in the indoor fifty-metre pool at the Health & Wellbeing Centre off the High Street Mall. Recently turned sixty-seven, swimming three times a week for the past ten years, and even though fully retired now – two years ago with all the time in the world – he's still doing his laps at five-thirty am, as soon as the pool opens. The lifesaving staff, rolling out the non-slip mats, set their clocks by the old geezer and laugh at his daily standard joke: *Rolling out the red carpet for me, luv?* ... Yet Roma's pinball chant is wrapped like a fluttering banner around the twisted, burned-out hulk of a wheelchair with the two welded, gaping red and black skeletons that are still lodged in his chest – as they have been for most of his adult life. He can hear her singing now as, half-way through his twenty laps, the luminous clock on the giant screen hanging over the pool – that same clock he's seen for the past one thousand five hundred swims – those nervous digital numbers wobble and expand, glow into his face with such ferocity that he waves to swat them away, but his hand – like a ghost – slips through the foot-high numbers of hours, minutes and seconds; and the white-clad nurse, just out of focus, lifts her hand and points a long finger at the clock to remind Abel that it isn't counting down his laps but the seconds and minutes he has left to live, and Abel feels the warm comfort of the final solution to the scorched wheelchair embedded in his chest that

1

it will all, finally, be over. He'll be able to expunge that burned relic with the fused skeletons, and the lingering scorched smell, and mercifully and conclusively, Roma – still humming *pull the pin, hear the ping, silver ball bounce and ding* – will lift her fingers off the plastic flippers and allow the silver ball to 'drain', and it'll be game over, man. Finally he'll slip off the playfield into eternal peace as he'd half-wished while driving back from The Shelter; where the avocado-clad people – clapping and singing – had marched up to meet him, as his best friend George quite rightly quoted from Macbeth: *as I stand my watch upon the hill I looked down towards Birnam, and anon methought, the wood began to move …* But no, the ball is punched back into the playfield: *You're not getting off that easily, mate.* As the clock relentlessly advances, Abel whacks away the pulsing numbers, swipes through them again and again, buries his face in the water to drown that walking forest image, Shangri-La consumed by the inferno of Hades … and he starts lap eleven, working steadily, swinging and kicking, head rotating, his breath is forced, the realisation surges through him: his retirement tranquillity is over, no longer will he and Pamsy meet their neighbours for a drink and bite at the pub on Monday nights, nor will he attend the U3A lectures on Tuesday arvo, or babysit grandkids on Wednesday, or go to the bowling club on Thursdays, or help out at Welfare House cooking up a storm for the mates and dearies – NO, no way, that life is now terminated, the white-clad nurse points out, leaning back and sipping her coffee … The confounded clock clutches at his face with the suction of an octopus; Abel heaves, instead of his usual seal-like turn, grasping, treading water, trying to rip off the clock stuck to his face; the changing numbers invade his body like parasites, wedge in his throat, throb ominously in his left arm, press down in his chest atop the charred, gaping vestige ... The other barrel-chested man in his lane stops swimming and points at Abel and the white-clad nurse's spirit announces: *You can't exit yet, mate – have you given a full account of yourself?* Abel smacks at the apparition again – *be gone* – but not only doesn't she disappear, she shimmers, tormenting him, refusing to come into focus, just as the black whale – a woman in glistening black and white striped bathers – raises one hand and comically echoes the nurse's question: *Have you given a full account of yourself?* The women who swim breaststroke side by side cease their chatter to tread water, and like two parrots point at him and ask Abel the very same thing, and the blonde, blue-eyed lifeguard – in her baggy blue shorts, red polo with 'LIFEGUARD' on the front – looks at him and misses the socket in her belt, her small water bottle takes ages to majestically float sideways to the floor while her lips move: *Have you given a full account of yourself, Abel?* A stack of kick-boards, dropped by another lifeguard, silently tumble to the tiled floor – Abel counts them one by one, a total of nine – gracefully bounce back up before settling to the ground ... Breathing is strained, the numbers viral inside him, and his right palm itches like crazy. The overcooked wheelchair and skeletons threaten to break out of his chest to make their public debut, as a third lifesaver, running, airborne, glint of metal cylinder under his arm, is on Abel at the speed of lightning, and the giant pool hangar descends on Abel's face as thick steam blows at him, swirling in his face, dampening his vision. Shapes float in and out before they can be identified; scrambled versions of his name hang in the air, and the nurse whispers, *Not yet, mate ... have you given a full account of yourself? ...* In the foggy mist multiple Romas – at ages seven, seventeen and twenty-seven – whip back their coiled black hair, bend over pinball machines, pull plungers back, and shoot silver balls out into the playfield humming, *Pull the pin, hear the ping, silver ball bounce and ding ... Keep control, flip it back to spin and thwack ...*

Breathing is less laboured, and the pains have settled to an irritating niggle. Wet nostalgia runs down his windscreen like racing tadpoles; no exhilaration can rival that of being back inside his Mini, the excitement machine, surrounded by swirling steam (an embryo cocooned in its mother's womb) ... Everything soft and warm, working perfectly, and lacking any application on his behalf, he's heading where he wants to be ... *Ahhhhh*, Abel breathes deeply, the back-seat sex smells still as pungent as in the excitement machine's heady years; Abel rests his hands on the leather-covered steering wheel, what fun he had in that striped little car, but the voice *Abel ... Abel ... Abel* calls out again; Roma interrupts, bending down, sideways grin, gripping the plunger and pulling it back, *Come back to me once more, Abel, then I'll let you go ... DING.* The steaming excitement machine shoots off and even though he knows he'll need to bounce off countless solenoid jet bumpers in the pinball playfield before he can reunite with Roma – just the prospect of being with her again, to hold her, just hold her, one more time in that brightly lit basement – his eyes are ablaze!

4

The steaming excitement machine stops in the small street outside his house, the first house he can remember; Abel reclines in the warm cocoon, amid the swirling steam, and a panorama kicks in, no projection required; not only does it not deny the images to him, it plasters them on his face like a moving screen. The badly worn picket fence, white paint flaked off years ago, flat plywood posts hanging off the corroded metal strip, all so familiar that Abel runs his finger along the sharp tip of a rusty nail and pricks his skin; a trickle of blood but no pain, and in fact he smiles, breathing in the intoxicating gardenia perfume of his mother's much-loved bushes, and the gate swings back as it has countless times before and the tall lounge-room windows zoom all the way into the little striped Mini excitement machine to seek Abel. The afternoon's bright sun tickles the plate glass and old Abel laughs as he well recalls this favourite time of day for young Abel, the hour he has to himself, between returning from school and his mother bringing home his twin sisters from kinder. Inside the house it's cool and serene – a creative environment – young Abel sits on the floor surrounded by his wooden blocks, hands working feverishly, on a hot-to-trot mission, eyes burning with plans to build one massive structure using every block that his father has made him since the day he was born, an ambitious plan as his massive collection fills several boxes – square wooden blocks of all sizes, ranging at least a dozen vibrant colours, hand crafted and meticulously painted – quite the logistical challenge – then the highlight, the anticipated crowning glory – that Daddy home from work will glow with pride at the finished project:

Good job, son, Abel my boy, give yourself a pat on the back ...
And Abel, laughing, would do just that, stand up, pat his
own back, right hand over left shoulder, just as he'd done
since he was a toddler and Dad would laugh and hug him
– old Abel slaps away the father images still ahead of
young Abel, time enough to suffer them later – focuses
back on young Abel, a tray with a glass of lemonade and
several chocolate teddy-bear biscuits, against his mother's
instructions to snack on cheese and fruit in this gap time
after school, but Abel instead follows his Granny Annie's
advice. Much to his mother's chagrin, after any meal at
Granny Annie's, she would produce a large round blue
tray with lamingtons, chocolate teddy bears, Tim Tams,
and white and pink meringues, and introduce it thus,
A plate of sweeties to balance out the nasties of life ... Next to
the afternoon's provisions lies the other protagonist of
this performance, Wags, his dog, casting silent, longing
glances at the biscuits, as only a big poodle bitser with
floppy ears and brown-black curly coat can ever do.
Occasionally, Abel tosses the begging black eyes a chocolate crumb, which the dog scoops in mid air, then lies
down, one eye half open, scrutinising his master's move-
ments ... Yes sir, old Abel smiles, in every possible way a
perfect afternoon scenario – no matter what repugnant
jet bumpers lie ahead on this playfield – the block building
is inspirational, young Abel is well into establishing a
solid foundation for his planned gigantic 'city' blocks
structure, crawling around the impressive formation,
adding blocks here and there, when Wags's head snaps up,
his ears rise, and he jumps, barks, then takes off, and
a moment later the flap bangs on the kitchen's doggy

door … Hmmm, Abel stops the structure's foundation work and cocks his head to one side for sounds of the dog's return; it's highly unusual for Wags to take off until the biscuit supply has been exhausted, and even back in the car, watching this 3D reality show, old Abel's stomach begins to churn … *Abel … Abel …* his name is called again, but he fixates on young Abel once more as the boy chooses a few more blocks to balance onto the structure, but the serenity of the afternoon has been broken, Wags should've been back by now. Young Abel meanders outside, the piercing orange disc rotates warmth into the boy's chest – old Abel recoils against the hazard notice plastering that young torso, but young Abel is of course oblivious to any omen as he calls for his dog several times, then hears him barking in the distance. Abel calls him again, louder, and when Wags doesn't appear Abel's face firms; this disobedient dog needs to be read the riot act. He jumps on his bike and pedals furiously into the street, dragging the potent gardenia-scent cloak right past the parked grey and black excitement machine with old Abel in it, then swings into a small passage, and comes out in the hilly nature reserve that runs for miles behind the row of houses … The sight of the reserve fills old Abel with the warm and fuzzies; swamped by the adventures with Wags exploring that bush, playing flat-out chasey, climbing trees, smashing birds' eggs for the dog to lick … but the best time of all, on weekends with Dad, the three of them exploring for hours, setting rabbit traps and wandering deep into the bush, sharing discussions on wildlife, the weather and the landscape, Dad's large backpack yielding all treasures from a blanket to ham sandwiches, Tim Tams and even a well-wrapped meaty bone for Wags, not that that'd stop him, Wags would jump up mid-picnic to chase a kangaroo, returning puffed and empty-jawed, collapsing at their feet, head tucked … *Never mind, Wagsie*, Dad'd laugh, *you tried your best, give yourself a pat on the back, mate* … Abel'd jump up and pat the dog's back and they'd all laugh, including Wagsie … But the best time of all was when Dad took him and Wags camping in the reserve, when they'd leave early morning straight after a hearty eggs-and-bacon breakfast, all carrying backpacks including the dog – Dad insisted that Wags contribute to carting the rations, so Mum sewed a small harness that strapped onto Wags's back like the rescue dogs in the Alps – and they'd wander until they reached the bubbling creek where they set up camp in what seemed like their private reserve. But no matter the heavenly state of the camping site, this was truly an *Ithaca* journey – Dad told him the story of the journey to the mythical island of Ithaca; it wasn't so much about the destination, but more the expedition – the adventure of getting there. Keeping a strong mind to reject imaginary monsters trying to scare them, concentrating on celebrating every step; nothing could touch them. Old Abel sees the father and son tramping through the bush, the boy stomping the dry leaves to a drumbeat of laughter, the white clouds drifting across the treetops as though on a conveyor belt, the sun spiking down turning the green leaves to shimmering gold. Leprechauns – from his school storybooks – with green top hats and orange beards grin at young Abel from behind the bushes. But the best – the highlight of this journey – was just before they got to the creek, they'd pass through an area of thick grass and high, dense trees, and since it was always about midday, the sun'd be directly overhead and shining down through the tall timber canopy in a cone-like shape to form a sparkling, sun-drenched cathedral. Father and son would exchange a conspiratorial grin, sharing the silent excitement of walking through this hushed bush space into their private world beyond, knowing that once they passed through their shimmering basilica nothing could touch them. They'd stomp loudly to announce their arrival to the local leprechaun population, then stop quietly to hear the stomping reply. Then, when they'd leave on their way back, once through the thicket, Dad'd make a 'locking the gate' motion, hiding the pretend key under a log for Abel to fossick for on their next appearance. In the reserve they'd spend the day fishing and exploring, then sleep, the two of them, snugly in sleeping bags inside the low tent, Wags wedged between them, but the funniest was that Wags, a strict meat-eater, succumbed to nibbling at the fried fish Dad had caught, not at all perturbed by the two humans' teasing remarks – *what wuss dog eats fish and chips, we won't tell your mates, Wagsie* ... Here again old Abel is forced to edit out that last camping trip that negated all that came before, when the journey to Ithaca was plagued by giant cannibals and Cyclops and angry Poseidon; young Abel's thoughts unable to block out these monsters, his youthful soul saw them stalking and threatening behind every tree and bush ... But that calamity is still a long way off as, buoyed by these earlier bonding adventures through the light-house cathedral, young Abel on his bike is zigzagging up the long incline through the huge trees and bushes of the nature reserve – the bike floats on a cushion of air like Aladdin on his magic carpet – but this isn't the case for old Abel who trembles as he calls out to the boy with his entire being, *Abel, come back*, but his steamy bellowing only merges with the pestering – female, soft yet determined, but otherwise unidentifiable – voice calling out behind him, just as frantically, *Abel, come back*. On top of the hill the boy stops dead on his bike, slanting sideways, one foot thrown down, he sits frozen, mesmerised, the brutal sun blanking out the horizon; he hears a hurricane-like roar before he sees it, the mighty bushfire front racing up the hill towards him, flames higher than the trees, chewing and snapping all in their path. Black–red smoke rolls relentlessly forward like surf; a branch, whipped up by the hot wind, lands smouldering at the bike's front wheel, the tiny flames hiss and spark, turning the brown wood black and red … As he watches his own reflection in the approaching wall of flames he forgets about his dog, loses the will to move, as the heat sears his shirt-front and browns his knees – sticking out of his shorts – like warm toast, cinders prick his face like hot beestings, the stench of his own singeing hair and his scorching eyelashes hits and his chest heaves upwards, expanding with the incubating heat. A giant, frantic-eyed, flaming kangaroo bounds right at him, its next manic hop will no doubt land right on top of the boy and his bike – the view is interrupted as a yellow plastic arm dripping greasy water plucks the boy from his bike like a scythe felling a restored soul – the boy, still fixated on the flaming kangaroo, is carried backwards, bouncing like a log in a smooth yellow armpit, he watches as the animal buckles and falls on his bike, both consumed by flames. Finally the boy is flung onto the floor of a metal cabin then bounced on his side, wedged between two wet, yellow plastic suits, to the sound of frantic shouting overridden by blaring sirens, the distance breaking away from the heat … and after the truck stops and he's wrapped in a wet towel and given a water bottle … Old Abel swallows hard, only now is he suddenly burning up with thirst, as the boy gulps down the amazing water and catches his reflection in a truck's side mirror – a little black, brown and red savage in charred clothing remnants, with tufts of charcoal hair so hilarious that the boy giggles – white teeth on parade in a blackened face – an image he'll well recall so many years later as he stares into a similar mirror with Roma's blackened daughter, Acacia, in her charred pink tutu by his side – and Abel in the car collapses back into the seat with the taste of that cool, life-saving water on his lips and reclines, exhausted, but there's no Roma touching his face with those faith-healing hands, and the melted wheelchair and two gaping skeletons are just around his next few DING, CLANG, BING pinball heartbeats and Abel has a revelation: the game's rules state you can't escape from what's already happened, because once you're plunged into the playfield, ricocheted to and fro, Roma's hands gripping the flippers will not allow you to drain, until you have definitely and com-prehensively, given a full account of yourself. Old Abel catches a glimpse from the side of his eye, a ghostly nurse shimmers in the back seat, arms reaching out, whispering *Abel, Abel, come to me …*

Abel succumbs to the pressure on his body, his arms, legs and chest are being pummelled, but it doesn't distract him as he rolls towards his next destination. This new house is double storey, surrounded by a wild bougainvillea garden/fence – thorny vines with masses of green leaves and bright magenta flowers hang over Abel's head like collapsed umbrellas – the concrete footpath at his feet, his scratched initials (AJM) still clearly visible, saturated with the memory of the night after the footpath had been poured, Dad waking him with finger across his lips, draping sleepy Abel in a dressing gown, sneaking the two of them out the window, coaching Abel with screwdriver to inscribe the letters for posterity ... But more than the nostalgia of running his old finger over the dusty grey initials, the wild bougainvillea zooms into Abel's face with the force of a curved 3D screen, so real that he breathes in the sharp tang of the magenta flowers as he bends over, and slips though the well-trodden gap between the bushes, contorting his shoulders to avoid the thorns; a few yards away Mum and Dad standing, smiling, one arm around each back, Mum holding a glass of white wine, Dad a beer, facing Bernie and Margaret, their best friends, smiling the same way, standing in the exact position holding drinks, between them assorted meat sizzles on the barbecue ... The six kids of the two families torment a brand new kitten, Ginger, until she crawls under the trampoline to get some peace, then the two older boys kick the footy and the four younger kids jump like crazy on the trampoline to further annoy the kitten; the ideal afternoon's itinerary recites itself minute by domestic-blissful minute. The sun burns young Abel's shirtless back, but there's no talk of sunscreen, the mixed grill impregnates the air with hunger as the four adults don sunglasses, cuddling kissing, drinking, teasing and whispering risqué jokes … Old Abel wishes he could peel back young Abel's eyes to see and predict the coming fall: Bernie's longing scan of Mum's mini-skirted legs, Mum's clandestine thighs chafing in reply, a tweak of her bra, Bernie's horsey snort acknowledging signal received, Dad's … no, old Abel can't do this, even after all these years, he can't find the heart to damage young Abel's memory. If he takes this perfect image away, what does the young boy have left? A childhood minus Dad, Wags and the forest reserve camping trips? No, he leaves the boy be, leaves him to remember that rosy, shiny, secure afternoon, the height of his blissful familyhood, stretched to unfold frame by frame over the next few months like time-lapse photography, as the sky slowly pales and dawn approaches – for another bonus sunshiny day in an additional season, as all the boy's sunshiny memories are – old Abel's foreboding cramps are back, this time accompanied by a sunburned back – he cannot shield young Abel any longer. Abel, weighed down by his giant school bag rubbing on sunburn, ignores his dizziness and heaving stomach to drop his sisters off at junior school, accepting their hugs – *One more squirrel hug, Ali* – copying Dad's morning routine, *Go on, that's enough now, off you go my two little squirrels, the teacher is waiting* and off they strut, primed and jovial … then he drags himself home from school in the mid morning, pulls himself up the long, curved banister, drops his bag on the carpet and rushes to the toilet to puke his guts out. Now copying his mother Abel presses his open palm to his forehead, then another dash to the loo to shake and shudder and dry retch some more, he goes downstairs, and phones his mother's work but is told that she too is sick, and won't be at work that day … *What are the odds of that, hey?* … Abel struggles to his room, strips, puts on his pyjamas, buttons them up crookedly and takes his temperature. Picturing his mother he times the three minutes on his bedside clock, struggles to stay awake then checks the reading, he's burning up, over forty degrees. He crushes two Aspro in a glass of water, drinks down the bitter mixture, then with relieving sigh tucks himself into bed … how proud will Mum be with how he's looked after himself, and his sisters, when he was so incredibly unwell …

Sick, hot and nauseated, Abel wakes up to his mother's screams: *Oh my god … oh my god … I can't take much more, please, please, stop, oh my god* … Abel drags himself out of bed, groggily pulls up his pyjama pants and holding them tight tiptoes into his parents' bedroom, his mother's screams now fever pitch. *My god,* thinks groggy Abel trying to shake the sleep, *she's being attacked by a robber,* and picks up his pace, but the door slightly ajar reveals something unexpected: in the reflection of the full-length mirror he can see his mother lying on the bed, legs spread wide, and his naked father, on all fours on the carpet, his head stuck in between Mum's legs; Mum throws her head from side to side: *Oh my god … OH MY GOD* … on the floor next to Dad is their kitten, Ginger, trying to catch the teasing, dangling strap of Mum's garter belt … But wait – Abel's body stiffens, he looks away then back, rubs his scratchy eyes letting go of the pyjamas that tumble to his ankles – it isn't Dad at all, this back is too hairy and too white … then … confirmation! The man lifts his head and speaks, Abel's burning eyes snap open – it's not Dad's voice, not Dad at all, it's Bernie, Margaret's husband: *Your cunt drips honey, honey.* Then complete confirmation: Bernie's trademark horse laugh: *I could lick this sweetness forever …* Old Abel in his excitement machine is swamped with the realisation: his lifelong aversion to honey was hatched that afternoon, but honey is the last thing on young Abel's mind as Mum, with a sudden twist of head, sees a wedge of Abel's stooped, half-naked reflection in the long mirror. Then as though a director had yelled *ACTION!* Mum, with a much louder *OH MY GOD*, bolts upright; Bernie, head clamped, is thrown off and lands sideways crushing kitty Ginger beneath him, and Abel shoots back to his room, jumps into bed, and hides under the blankets … and old Abel in the car scrambles under a blanket of lingering shame, massaging that long-ago-healed sunburn … if he could re-write the game rules he'd have gladly suffered that severe sunburn for the rest of his life, if Ginger could have lived, and Mum and Dad had stayed as they were on that sunny Brady Bunch barbecue afternoon … And when Jill, so many years later, made him that once-in-a-lifetime offer of dumping *Abel* and becoming *Jackson*, that boyhood bedroom image had played foremost on his adult mind – that fever-dazed boy standing, forever clutching his pyjama pants – the steel ball of his life bouncing off in an irretrievable direction.

Young Abel tries to picture smiley faces on the white clouds drifting overhead, everyone is talking and laughing and wearing nice clothes including him, but he can't embrace the high spirit and in fact resents the clouds, *such heartless happiness!* and old Abel, sitting in his steamy car, ignoring the white female phantom calling from behind, feels just as reticent, but the two Abels do have one solid ally in this sense of foreboding, the only tight-lipped one not openly celebrating is Granny Annie: she isn't examining clouds, or dragging feet like her grandson, but is in fact standing *too* still, losing track of what we call movement she watches Abel from the edge of the celebrating crowd as he intently investigates the drifting cumulus masses, and then – as though it is at all possible – the scene on the wide, high front steps of the town hall is about to get even happier – Brady Bunch eat your heart out – Mum and Bernie come out, clutching hands, smiling and waving to everyone, and so, exactly, do Dad and Margaret. Mum and Margaret, in bright dresses, carrying bunches of flowers, and Dad and Bernie, in suits and ties and brown shoes, part as couples, Dad and Bernie shake hands and clap on backs, Mum and Margaret kiss, then the two couples reform, so that family and friends, gathered along the steps, line up to hug them and throw rice and white flowers, which signals to Granny Annie to finally recall her mobility – she walks over to Abel and his sisters who hang about on the sidelines – the sisters watching Abel watching nothing – and Granny Annie corrals Abel, Rose and Mary and pushes them forward to hug their parents' knees, but that presents a logistical problem: their Mum's knees are next to Bernie's, and Dad's knees are next to Margaret's; Mum twists sideways to kiss Bernie, Dad, copycat, kisses

Margaret, then again Mum kisses Margaret, and Dad and Bernie clap each other on the back, so blissful that they'd plum forgot they'd already done that five minutes earlier; young Abel is bewildered and wonders: *Why are they giving each other a pat on the back? What have they done to deserve that?* But the boy can't dwell too long on this unwarranted behaviour, he's too busy reviewing in his head the barriers he'd implanted there to reject Mum and Dad's recent *talks* with him and his two sisters in the last few weeks – yep, the shields are up and intact and he has no trouble dumping those one-way dialogues straight into the rubbish bin … Mum and Dad, in cheerful tears, had smiled and kissed and cuddled him and Rose and Mary, but what they said fell like sharp, dead words, without even a touch of life or colour; Abel slinking through those thorny words, contorting right and left and not one syllable pricked his skin like the thorny bougainvillaea; his sisters refused to understand what their parents were talking about, looking to their big brother for orientation or total rejection; their silence held together until the three kids were alone in his room, even as Abel dragged his two sisters onto his bed, hugged them and cried and they cried because he was crying – whimpering like injured puppies – because Abel had his finger across his lips for silence and his two sisters would do anything, absolutely anything, for Abel – with big teary eyes and fingers across their lips they stared at him in the dark room, and knew that things were bad, if their superhero brother was crying, things were very bad indeed. For the past couple of weeks he'd secretly listened behind the lounge-room door to the argy-bargy of his parents and their best friends, Bernie and Margaret, their meetings over many hours, at first harsh, accusing, raised, angry voices, but then softer, reconciliatory declarations, even laughter, signed off by clinking glasses and Bernie's horsey laugh, all cumulating in this mongrel town hall gathering. Abel's sisters' regimented lead-following on his bed is no different now on the town hall steps as the three stand in a row, with dead arms, sneering. Too much hair ruffling and arm squeezing had followed the *talks* that only served to confirm to young Abel that this was all bullshit, they'd been sold a dud, and he pictured the worst of all scenarios: the nightmare of Dad, Bernie, Abel and John, Bernie's son, on the forest's grassy earth, squeezed inside one sleeping bag in the small tent, but he can't dwell too much on that dreadful image as Bernie bends down and firmly shakes his hand and neighs: *I love you like a son … we'll have some great times together …* Shrinking away from Bernie, Rose and Mary squint up at their older brother and pull down on his arms to explain to them what's going on, but there's no interval to clarify the proceedings as Dad – their real dad – smile widespread, leaves Margaret and comes over, kneeling down to Abel's level, and looks into his son's eyes and his lips move but his words jam up like a train at a dysfunctional railway crossing; after some coughing, Dad's words make a clunky noise inside Abel's head, but the boom gate stays down. Rose and Mary finally loosen their grip on their older brother as they climb onto Dad's knees and hang from his neck like they're drowning and he's a lifesaver, but Margaret turns out to be the real lifesaver in this shipwreck as she comes over and untangles the two crying girls and rescues her new husband who's fixated trance-like on Abel, the young boy silently stepping back with dropped chin, while Granny Annie presses her arms to her side so as to stay motionless again, because any movement – even the minimum – might unleash punches to her son's head … There's a party of course, the six kids sitting together in their best clothes at their own table – if this was meant as a display of solidarity, it actually has the reverse effect: John stabs Abel with dirty looks for stealing his dad, and Abel kicks him under the table with his new solid black shoes, John's eyes fill with silent tears but he more than deserves the pain, because Abel's stolen dad is a million times better than John's dumb dad who does nothing but laugh like a horse and squash cats to death.

The adults eat, drink and laugh, ignoring the catastrophe in front of them; these two new unions are jinxed from their genesis; why, otherwise, would Granny Annie have placed on the long white tables – like stepping stones to salvation or doom – plates with her usual selection of sweeties to balance out the nasties of life? His twin sisters hang back, their older brother hasn't reached out to the central offerings either, and the girls suspect that indeed there are no good times to celebrate here. Mum, watching from the head table with a slowly shrinking smile, leaning forward, fingers nervously strumming the table while watching her mother-in-law's plate distribution as though instead of deliverance these are indeed rumblings signalling an impending disaster – the same mum who never stops lecturing about the evils of Granny Annie's *sugar* plates – gets up, takes a plate in each hand, walks over to their table and extends them as a peace offering, but to Abel it's more like a stab in the heart. Abel's eyes look up from the hovering plates to his mother's crinkled-smile face, then slumps; no way in hell is he accepting a substitute prize for their stolen life, even the most gigantic plate of sweeties will not balance out the nasties this time. Rose and Mary, both hands stopped while reaching out to their mother's offering, drop their hands to the white tablecloth with a soundless thump that makes Mum shudder, powerless before her kids' united rejection.

Mum turns to Granny Annie and locks into a moment's standoff that lingers for hours – as though blaming her as the leader in this resistance movement – and while Mum's hands shake as though about to smash these hateful sweetie plates on Granny Annie's white lace hat, *twaddle* rings in Abel's head and it's about as close to mirth as he'll get on this calamitous day, and for many days to come, repeating in his head: *twaddle, twaddle, twaddle* ... which had been Granny Annie's reply when Mum had laid the separation and remarriage plans on her, *twaddling* it right into her daughter-in-law's face without flinching and Abel, hiding behind the barely closed lounge-room door, had to cup his mouth not to laugh out loud ... *twaddle,* Granny Annie said – *twaddle,* he told Mary and Rose who were hiding in his room still hoping for a miracle, naively believing that their last hope, Granny Annie, could change the outcome of this calamity ... And in a way she had as Abel understands that *twaddle* is indeed a victory of sorts ... Later that night of the double re-marriage, in the bed in Granny Annie's house, Rose and Mary twig a little as to their changed circumstances, they sneak into Abel's room as he's lying on his back in the bed he'd last slept in a year ago when Mum and Dad had gone for a holiday with Bernie and Margaret. Now the four of them had gone away again but it's not the same, as was made plainly clear at the overheard drunken jibes at the party earlier: *Careful, don't call out the wrong name when the action starts … best friends split up, marry the others, and are still best friends … so civilised – all you need is love, right?* And the funniest, totally beyond Abel's comprehension, was that his parents – the original ones – laughed heartily with all the others, but young Abel has the last laugh now as in bed at Granny Annie's he sneers at his mother's sharp parting look, refusing to accept her spiked accusation that weaves its way like a homing missile through the merrymakers, aimed directly at Abel's forehead: *It's all your fault. If you had just gone to school like you were supposed to …* All good and well being brave and mocking his mother earlier, but now, in bed, Rose and Mary, nervy about Abel's long silence, try to revive their brother's old playfulness, climbing on Abel's stomach and asking him to make them bounce; Abel – albeit, silently – bounces them as long as he can but when he stops Mary asks, *Ali, why is Dad leaving us to live with Margaret and John and Aaron and Cindy? … Ali*, Rose echoes, *Why is Bernie coming to live with us?* Abel hopes his sisters know that discovering Mum and Bernie's deed isn't the same as actually doing it – but how can he explain this disaster to these two little girls perched on his stomach holding back tears? Abel will have to cope, he's old enough, but his sisters are lost in a broken family, and he can't explain to them why … He thinks back to a time when everything still made sense, a moment captured in a framed photo by his bedside, the family's talisman. A few months after his baby sisters were home from hospital, Abel had snuck into their room and scratched their faces. Their screams woke up Mum and Dad and, when severely reprimanded, Abel had whimpered, *Why can't we go back to being just Abel, Mum and Dad and Wags like before?* Mum had hugged and kissed her son, pointing out that they were now five Marvins plus dog, and taken a self-timed family photo for posterity, Abel smiling through tears, head wedged between the scratched-up twins, Mum pressed on one side holding a sign that said 5×M+D (conveying five Marvins plus dog) and Dad on the other holding puppy Wags. Abel tries to think how he'd photograph – let alone explain to his sisters – the new bastard-mix of families, but he can't, no iconic scribbling could ever capture this mess. After that first night at Granny Annie's, whenever Abel lay flat on his back in bed, he felt his two sisters' ghosts clutching his neck and bouncing on his stomach and heard their little confused voices and he'd squirm; his worst predictions proved so painfully accurate, their old life, that close bond between Abel and his father, had disappeared just as Wags had in that long ago bushfire and so had his sisters' verve in a stable family … 5×M+D was no more.

Second week back from their group honeymoon, Abel stays with Dad and Margaret and John, while Aaron and Cindy stay with Mum and Bernie and Rose and Mary, the weekend enterprise smacking of disaster from its onset, as the minute Mum drops Abel off, Dad waves a little too fervently to his ex-wife then introduces Abel to the new dog, Sunshine, a dumb golden retriever with watery grey eyes. Of course Abel has been many times to this house – they were best friends of his parents, weren't they? – but on past visits he'd torn into John's room, the two boys closing the bedroom door to keep the four smaller brat siblings outside, then checking out any new toys or gadgets, spending the rest of the time chasing, hiding and playing – why, he knows that house as well as his own. But today he feels as though he's dragged shit in on his heels, leaving stinking smudges on anything he touches. The sojourn to John's room lasts no more than a few silent minutes, the door staying open behind him, John, mute, slouching on the floor. When he can stand it no longer Abel goes into the lounge and switches on the TV; from the corner of his eye he sees that Margaret is about to object to midday TV-watching, but Dad gives a short sharp nod to leave Abel be and he sits, watching for hours, not as a visitor, not even a stranger, or a friend, just an un-belonging person, all he sees on the TV screen are his two sisters watching in silence at the breakfast table as the sleepover announcement is floated by Mum. Not one word, not a hug, not even a crying *Ali, take us with you* … especially Mary, accusing Abel of desertion with each fired glance … Later with a rah, rah, rah Abel is recruited to drag a spare mattress into John's room, to sleep on the floor next to his new 'brother' and as soon as Abel clamps eyes shut, he sees Mary again in his bedroom doorway, watching him pack his pyjamas and spare shirt into his backpack, making a mess of the folding under her silent scrutiny. She's mute again, mouth pursed, no way is she going to cry, her *Ali* should know better than to heartlessly desert her. Rose is too upset to come into his room, bad enough that Dad has deserted them, now Abel abandons his 'two little squirrels' to the enemy. On his way out past the girls' room, he *feels* Rose scrunched up on her bed. On the floor mattress in Dad's new house when Dad finally comes in to rub his back and tuck him in as he did years ago at home, Abel turns his face away.

The next morning, early, after a tasteless breakfast, Dad can't wait to pack the two boys and new dog into the car and drive to the nature reserve and park in the street next to *their* house, so congenially planned and executed, that smiling Mum comes out and hugs Dad and laughing Bernie comes out and shakes hands, and Rose and Mary come out and, wailing, clutch Daddy's legs and won't let go … Finally, in a team effort, they manage to disentangle Dad from his crying daughters and then it's the moment Abel has dreaded and is now seared into his brain – worse than scratching their baby faces: his sisters look up at him angrily, Mary slowly mouths *I hate you, Ali* with a cold and fierce stab way beyond her years – more reminiscent of Mum – an expression Abel will remember as clearly as an alien sighting years later when Mary, as payback, wrecks his life and hers … Meanwhile the man and two boys and dog shoulder their backpacks and Dad hoists the tied bundle of two tents, but Sunshine can't manage his doggy backpack, trembling in shock, and at first Dad laughs and teases Sunshine, but after the tenth slip down of the pack Dad just takes it off and hangs onto it … Abel walks in silence, kicking loose branches while Dad explains to John the adventure's procedure, but he may as well explain it to his son too as this is a different bush reserve, this forest is dead and silent, the leprechauns having emigrated, this trudging journey to the magical island of Ithaca is populated by mythical Greek monsters, but they're half-hearted at best. The single eye of the Cyclops glares from behind trees, as intimidating as a paper cut-out. Bearded Poseidon waves his fist promising earthquakes and storms but Abel sneers, *Bring them on*. The tribe of giant cannibals raise themselves to attack positions, smacking their lips with hunger; Abel laughs in their faces … But this is nothing – mere kids' stuff – the real danger raises its hostile head when the three weary travellers plus dog get to the sparkling cone-shaped cathedral – Dad doesn't respect the occasion, this rite of passage to their private sanctuary has simply elapsed, *Not a sign of recognition. Not even a shared grin. How could he?* Abel's last hope – the expectation that once they passed through to their private, isolated world, all would revert to what it was *before* – is dashed … Abel drags himself to the creek, Mary's words *I hate you, Ali* weighing down his shoulders more than his backpack, and when they finally set up camp, even the fish refuse to cooperate, not one bites, whereas in previous trips Dad had to yell down into the water: *Take a number, you slippery sea-creatures …* Keeping up the charade they build the traditional campfire in the rocky space near the river, but there's nothing to cook, when a kangaroo hops by – as a last walk-on prop to save this melodrama – but Sunshine barely lifts his head, and Dad has to rev him up and launch him into the chase but the dog returns soon after not even a little puffed out – and what's worse, not showing the least bit of remorse, the dumb dog stands around watching them, Dad says: *Give yourself a pat on the back, mate, for trying, Sunshine* ... which is a bit over the top. Hiding his tears with his elbow, Abel grabs a fishing rod to have another go at this farce but the bloody fish won't cooperate even with the whimpering boy; even back home would be better, Abel could at least silently face off Mary's anger, justified as it was for not sharing Dad with her ... Finally night, they sleep in the two tents, Dad on his own and Abel with John who talks and farts in his dreams, but young Abel can't sleep anyhow, even if John slumbered like a non-farting angel, because before Dad clicks off his torch, he gives his son one long apologetic look, and both manage to just hold back tears. When Abel finally goes to sleep he chants in his head the usual mantra he's repeated silently every night since that travesty of a wedding: *Mum is right, it's all my fault. It's up to me to set things straight. I must return life to what it was before I wagged school that bloody day just because I was a little bit sick.*

Bouncing around on the playfield, from jet bumper to turbo bumper to mushroom pumper to drop targets, kickers, slingshots, ramps and saucers, the scoring reels on the pinball machine's back glass kick over rapidly racking up time; it takes two years after that bungled camping trip before a chance to rebalance their lives falls into Abel's lap ... He plays with his monster yellow dump-truck on top of the stairs when the upstairs toilet is blocked. A heavy, impressive vehicle, over half a metre long and almost as high, and Mum is pleased: *Gosh, you haven't played with that old truck in years* ... the rare praise wafts over Abel's shoulder with no place to land, as Abel, on his knees, pushes the truck up and down the upstairs passageway, outside the toilet, alongside the bedrooms, making loud truck noises when it stops and starts at the imaginary traffic lights. Mary and Rose – under Mary's leadership estranged from him after he'd defected to the enemy – watch their brother's regression with suspicion, evaluating his crystal-hard eyes – the mood scares them … but old Abel in the car hums through the thick blanket of steam, short gasps of anticipation: that old yellow monster truck is leading Abel towards Roma, back arched, concentrating on the playfield, humming her childhood refrain: *Pull the pin, hear the ping, silver ball bounce and ding* … but at this stage it's still many pinnie bounces away from young Abel, as the truck has a prior mission cast in solenoid pings, in this old house, with old toilets, and an absent plumber with replacement parts a week away, so every afternoon after school, Abel plays with his large yellow vehicle along the same route on top of the stairs – one way, then the other – his sisters leaning out from their shared bedroom, staring silently, Mary's lip sneering; their traitorous brother can never restore balance to their out-of-kilter life. Then when the ball hits the right bumper, Bernie gets up in the middle of the night to use the downstairs toilet – as he does every night at least twice – Abel is waiting behind the linen cupboard, and silently launches the big yellow monster on its kamikaze mission along the top of the stairs, and dopey, hung-over Bernie trips over and tumbles headfirst down the long, curvy stairs without a smidgen of his horsey laugh.

The thinly-veiled white nurse hovers over Abel as he lies back in the steamy car, reliving Bernie's tumble and fall, her silent, irksome stare is asking as always, *Have you given a full account of yourself?* As Abel squirms, angry that he can't recognise her, she begins squeezing pressure and release on his hands; the 3D vision is unavoidable – pasted onto Abel's forehead – thumping bumping Bernie plummeting down the stairs. But he finds no residue in his psyche – this playfield is only so big and his chest has been scorched so long with the twisted relic of the melted wheelchair and the two gaping skeletons, there's no space left for Bernie's cathartic tumble. The white nurse nods and pushes him towards the pinball machine that has only the one supreme mission: to lead Abel to *Dame Gypsy-of-the-Romani*, Roma donning her cape of blue and green with the large red spoke wheel in the middle … a cape-wrapped bundle of laughing and teasing, long whipped jet-black hair. Abel does denial every day – dislodging the sound of Bernie's tumbling thump – as he does every time he crosses eye-beams with Mum – her eyes all accusation – silent blasts that cut him up and bleed him for days, even his own returning silent eye-volley of *I just rectified what I fucked up in the first place* doesn't placate Mum at all … going to the cops would be less traumatic … on top of that – even worse – not only does Dad not come back to live with them, he never again takes Abel camping, and Mum starts inviting boyfriends to sleep over, punishing Abel with yet more silent missiles: *It's your fault … you made me a widow slut …* Yet, strangely, Abel becomes thankful for his mother's stabs, the only snippet of her familiar personality … this new mum stranger in her loud, short skirts and lurid tops smells sickly sweet as though dunked in perfume, a much closer and much harsher health hazard than Granny Annie's plates of sugar. Mum shimmies inside her clothes as though a bead is lodged between her breasts and she intends on shaking it all the way down to fall out of her dress on the floor, provoking her man friend to comment: *When you move like that, baby, I want to throw you down and ram my dick inside your cheeky cunt*, and Mum knows Abel loiters outside the barely closed lounge-room door, like she wants him to hear the result of his actions: *There you go, Abel, this is what you made ...* The loitering has become a game of one-upmanship: Abel sneaks past in full view, Mum revs up her shimmying, Abel bounces on the trampoline and at the height of each bounce locks eyes with Mum, Mum's eyes alternate between boyfriend's face and bouncing son's head, a cynical smile rising on her face, her first-born can do nothing to alter the situation he has created. *Meow ... meow ... meow ...* Abel summons long-dead Ginger's ghost, confident Mum can read his lips. But the victory is marred because on this particular occasion, his sisters have followed him and heard Mum's boyfriend, and since Rose and Mary are now old enough to understand about dicks and cunts, silent tears spring to Rose's eyes and Mary's daggers stab at Abel: *You did that, you turned our mother into a whore ...* Abel shrugs off Mary's accusations and engulfs Rose with his arms to protect the grown-up squirrel, and all three kids silently retreat from the gaping lounge-room door, escaping to the safety of Abel's room, even Mary – who hasn't been in there for years, since the camping desertion – the girls sit on the edge of the bed, their eyes all a-panic, so that there is no way that Abel can go out with his mates as planned and leave his sisters on their own, sunken-face Rose is liable to self-harm much worse than just a scratched face, and Mary will blame him again … Abel jerks his head *come on* and Rose is slow to respond but Mary jumps up all a-smile. On their way back to the lounge room the three kids let loose an avalanche of noises to telegraph their presence to Mum and boyfriend; *We're going out*, Abel announces and Mum gives a genuine smile, Abel is finally including his two sisters in his outside activities, plus she can take her latest boyfriend up on his offer … Old Abel watching the screen feels every forceful push as the grown boy dips down on his bike's pedals, the girls following behind on their bikes, the three kids heading to Abel's best mate's house, where two guys sit smoking on the house's front step, dumbstruck to see the three bike-riding Marvin entourage: *The wanker brought his sisters?* … Both Abels can read their surprise … *They're cool, Mum went out, couldn't leave them at home on their own* … Abel lights up as well, as the two mates shuffle and mooch around – these girls are old enough to be home on their own, old enough to do a lot more than that, Rose is a grown-up squirrel but Mary is now more of a fox – but then the mates decide to accept the package deal, his best mate puts it behind him and announces: *Oldies went to the pub in Mum's car. They won't be back for hours. I know where Dad's keys to the V8 are hidden …*

The two mates sit in the front, Rose and Mary sit in the back with Abel next to them, contemplating the seatbelts (he's never been in a car with back seatbelts), after a moment's hesitation Abel grumbles to the girls: *Put your seatbelts on*, the sisters exchange a glance, decide not to push their luck, then click the belts into place ... The kids drive to a burger joint, pool their money and stock up on burgers, chips and shakes, then drive to an empty parking lot, turn up the radio, open all four doors and tuck in, the boys drinking warm beer stolen from home and flicking cigarette ash out the open doors, and the girls gorging on flavoured milk. In the men's world of the empty factory complex the boys miss their usual banter about girls that they know – who, where, how and what they'd like to do to them, which girl *lets you go goal-to-goal* and which wastes time with arm-wrestling – but Abel shrugs, *What can I do?* ... Rose and Mary feel the heavy silence and know that they're in its centre; Rose glares at the charcoal factory complex with the silent, empty chimneys, but Mary eyeballs the two boys, catching their quick glances, challenging them to face off. On the way back the boys need to release some pent-up testosterone so the best mate – Mary's eyes stroking the back of his neck – drives too fast in his dad's hot car, taking back roads to avoid cops; they hit something and the car bounces up, the passengers yell, the driver swears *I'm fucking dead meat*, and tyres squeal to a halt. Jumping out they run back into the dark, towards a pitiful yelping dog; when they reach it, it scans the three boys asking them with silent, crazy eyes *Am I about to die?* ... Abel starts when his sisters grip his arms – he'd momentarily forgotten about them – he wants to shield their eyes but can't tear himself away from the bleeding dog ... *Looks just like Wags*, Rose whispers, digging her fingers into his flesh; Abel turns to stare at his sister in the dark – how the hell would she know? She was only a tiny tot when Wags disappeared during the bushfire … *Just like when Wags lay down and played dead*, Mary agrees – *Not bloody likely*, Abel thinks, but realises his sisters are referring to Wags's framed pictures in his bedroom, next to 5×M+D. His best mate returns from inspecting the car, *Dad'll kill me, side fender fucked* – Abel asks, *What are we going to do with the dog?* Now that his sisters have implanted Wags's image onto the injured dog he can't leave it to bleed so pathetically on the road. His best mate checks the boot: *There's no blanket.* Abel takes off his shirt, his two mates do the same; they clumsily bandage the dog but when they lever him up, he yelps and snaps at their hands. *We need to tie up his mouth*, a moment's hesitation, the three boys are already bare chested, Mary slips off her top and a long second later so does Rose. Rose's arms snap shut tightly across her bare chest – but not Mary, whose boobs are now well and truly burgeoning. The two mates are stunned. Abel blushes, it's been years since he's seen his two sisters topless, but Mary – *Geeze … let's do it*, Abel shakes himself and his mates out of their reverie, they pull Rose's top over the dog's face and they tie Mary's sleeves around the dog's neck, he looks like he's been to war … The dog yelps in heartbreaking pain as they place him in the boot, then they screech towards the vet in the town's centre and the three bare-chested guys carry the dog inside, then slip away without giving their names or details, driving with the lights off. In a nearby street they stop, turn on the radio, open all four doors, with great sighs they light up cigarettes, the dark starry sky signalling that the status quo has changed, they now have two topless girls among them ... Bare-chested Mary is offered a smoke and takes it without hesitation, flicking ash with the boys; Rose shakes her head, covers her chest and looks away ... *We'd better get back to your place*, Abel, red-faced, flinches at the snapped glances of his two mates at Mary's bare chest, floods with uncontrollable memories of Mum – he flicks away his half-finished smoke and tells everyone to hurry up ... His best mate loans them t-shirts for the ride home that look like mini dresses on the sisters, Mary wiggling as she slips hers on. A week later Abel can't resist a phone call to the vet – the dog has lost a leg but will survive – but the warm and fuzzy feeling for having saved a life lasts only about a year ... Mary gets pregnant; Abel's best mate is the father ... *Did you know this was going on?* Mum accuses Abel, with words, this time, well, he did and he didn't, if he hadn't taken the girls that night ... From Rose it's *If you hadn't taken us that night* – from Mary, *We're a team again, and this time I'm in your gang, Ali* ... But Mum has found legitimate leverage: *I thought you looked after your sisters.* All in all it hadn't been a good night out – sure, he'd saved the dog that didn't look anything like Wags, but he'd lost his two sisters and his best mate, who was of course barred from coming anywhere near Mary Marvin or her pimp brother ever again.

Just as scary as your first shag, right matey? Old Abel grins from the back seat of the driving instructor's car, one steering wheel in front gripped by the driving instructor, a big guy with motley-veined face, suffering a permanent hangover, young Abel gripping the other. On a dare with himself old Abel extends his right hand through the whirling fog but the steam sticks to his fingers like wet glue; the more he strains the further the front seats stretch out of reach ... *Been driving for two years, mate, this is just to get my licence* ... Scratch of swollen red nose, *But that other, first time, was terrifying, right?* – bloodshot eyes grin – *Those smooth young legs opening wide and the job is laid out to be done, right?* ... Scary or not, both Abels know that the first time was nothing notable; a few blind jabs, camouflaged by alcohol, cloaked in darkness beneath bushes, but the second time – a mammoth second time – was a lesson in itself, before obtaining that other licence – the one to know how to get women hot. But first things first, how he got here, with Granny Annie's help of course ... For the past few months, young Abel has been living with Granny Annie, in her big house raised on stumps, a heavy, brown wooden-beamed place, its hefty windows that take effort to lift, a place that groans with the wind, and smells from sweating wood in the summer. As a kid Abel's dad used to play hide and seek under the house with his siblings, amid huge heating ducts like bloated silver caterpillars; Dad once confided, *You can hear the grown-ups talk through the kitchen duct* ... little did he know – in those never-to-be-repeated bonding days – that his son would soon be in a similar position, and his parents had put him into exile under that big rambling house to listen in secret ... Bah, what *secrets?* ... Though it was only whispered at home, Abel knew all about Mary's abortion, gone for two days and when she returned, the house simply wasn't big enough for both of them, the bloody MCG would've been too small to accommodate the network of sharp accusing spider webs strung across all rooms, ensnaring and cutting him whichever way he moved; it was all Abel's fault. Everywhere Abel placed himself, everywhere he looked – he was lacerated, mostly in silence, as hardly anyone spoke about it when he was around. Muteness – an intolerable emperor – reined, even in his own room; so when Mum 'suggested' he spend some time with Granny Annie, it was not a proposition but a life sentence, a one-way sentence with no parole. When he was packing his things, Mary sneaked into his room so silently she gave him a jump: *All I wanted to do was join your gang, Ali.* She cried, *Dad was gone, I thought if I was your best mate's girlfriend you wouldn't leave me behind …* But Abel was no better than his dad. His father had left the family, now he was leaving his sisters to fend for themselves … That first day at Granny Annie's, after they take Abel's luggage upstairs to his dad's old room, Mum asks Abel to wait outside. On his way down the stairs Abel notices Granny Annie's round blue tray of sweeties (these days Granny Annie no longer hides her sweetie plates from Abel's mum, in fact she seems to flaunt them) – *Don't you start on your argy-bargy about too much sugar the way you've behaved* – and a storm of dark clouds brewing outside; following his Dad's tip Abel crawls under the house, but he must be a lot bigger than his father was as it's slow going and hot, squeezing around the heating ducts, peeling spider webs from his sweaty face, until he gets to the kitchen's heating vent, wishing the thunderstorms crackling and booming over the sea will delay their arrival long enough for Abel to hear: *I'm worried Mary will harm herself, if Abel stays at home* ... it takes Abel a confused minute to recognise who has spoken, it's Mum's new voice, flat and dry like brittle iron ... *Why does Mary blame Abel?* ... Distant clouds rumble ... *She doesn't, I do* ... *he should've looked after his sister better – So then, what's Mary's problem with her brother?* ... A long moment's silence as though someone has shut the vent ... *She fucked his best mate to please her brother, some hoo-ha about joining the gang* ... Abel, under the house, imagines Granny Annie giving his mother a hefty, silent rebuke; the hammering skies draw closer ... *Mary is ashamed that she wasn't careful enough, that she was too young and stupid* ... *Now she's ruined Abel's friendship, busted up their gang* ... *It's best that Abel lives over here for a while* ... silence for minutes ... *Mary can't look at her brother without crying* – *Bollocks*, Granny Annie's rebuke finds its voice, a step up from mere *twaddle* to *bollocks* – Abel's face breaks into a wide grin – *In my day it was the mother's responsibility to look after the young girls, not their siblings* ... Under-the-house Abel relaxes into his smile, bathes in it, not a word about the decadent tray of sweeties right in Mum's face ... Despite the joy, old Abel in the car still feels his younger body bristle with tension; the storm strikes just as Abel resurfaces from under the house, wading out into the wide front steps already flooded with water, Mum hugs his drenched spider-web-covered body, her farewell embrace sideways and short, not a word of caution to get out of the rain; that's Granny Annie's portfolio now as he stands, cowed, water cascading down his body like a park statue. Abel doesn't mind this transfer of jurisdiction, he loves his Granny Annie who's big all over, her body, her arms and her smile, so big that when Abel was little and learned about the workings of the heart, he had imagined a great big pink heart inside Granny Annie's chest beating like a pump, and whenever she'd hugged him, he could hear that hollow *thump … thump … thump …* Dripping with water he waits for that hug now; like clockwork, Granny Annie comes out and yells at him, *Don't be stupid, come in from the rain*, and as soon as he makes the front porch she strips his drenched, spider-webbed gear off, and in his jocks gives him one of her special hugs: *Sometimes, Abel, some things in life can't be exactly how you want them to be …* Even better, back inside the house – once Abel has dried and dressed himself and unpacked the three framed pictures next to his new permanent bed – the two of Wags and 5×M+D – he comes down the stairs and Granny Annie presses on Abel her large blue tray trumpeting a giant sweeties selection, then sits smiling, watching him crunch the white and pink meringues until he too waves a smile … *My best mate, we chased girls, we stole rabbits and cherries, nicked his Dad's shotgun and fired it in the bush at the birds …* How desperately old Abel wishes he could be back there with Granny Annie finishing the stories of love and loss swirling around in his head: *After Dad left, we carted my entire wooden block collection, you know the one made by Dad – massive – into the bush right in the middle of the cone light cathedral where we used to camp, built a giant structure and then we …* Abel can't help but grin … *then we – like a sacrifice to the forest monsters – blasted it all to hell with the shotgun, over and over, wooden splinters – red, yellow, purple, aqua – littering the forest floor, sparkling in the glistening rays and I only wish Dad was there to see the destruction ... years of his handiwork ...* Despite having left his family for good that day, Abel, in the back seat of the driving instructor's car, feels warm and cosy, Granny Annie's house always has that effect on him, and it isn't just the heating ducts, or the pound of sugar coating his gullet, Abel wants to wave away that nuisance name-calling from behind, constantly interfering with his life's screening, but both hands are imprisoned again by that squeezing and releasing pressure, so Abel concentrates on the end of that day, after the driving lessons, waiting in front of Granny Annie's house after school, to be picked up by Sergio, the proprietor and sole employee of Sergio's Impeccable Office Cleaning Service – Granny Annie got him this job through some charity organisation she helps out – and he's just in time as the yellow combi-van with the big black logos of an octopus-man with eight arms vacuuming, wiping, sweeping et cetera, pulls up; Abel slides back the side door and jumps in, and the van is off to its first job of the night, Abel assisting Sergio for four hours, three nights a week after school, and gets paid ten dollars in cash per night, that's thirty dollars a week, and in fourteen weeks he'll have enough for a deposit on the second-hand grey Mini with the black racing stripes he's been lusting after, and one-hundred-and-seventeen weeks after that, the car will be fully paid off, including interest, when two important events will coincide: Abel will leave school and be the show-off owner of a kick-ass Mini – Abel salivates at the thought of the googly-eyed girls as he'll cruise past in his impressive excitement machine with the radio blaring – the bonus of a third event, just as poignant: he'll be able to drop in on his sisters and take them for a spin whenever he wants to, and one of those days maybe Mary will start talking to him again and calling him *Ali* ... But this is all still in the future, as during those four hours of cleaning, Abel supplies the muscle for the older Sergio: he carries, pushes, lifts, shifts, moves, arranges and rearranges, while Sergio supplies the brains, expertise and polished mirror finishes; both man and boy are worn out at the end of the four hours, Abel has four days to rest, but poor Sergio works another three days with a different assistant.

Four weeks away from having the car deposit, Sergio gets sick and is hospitalised; after hearing the news, Abel, feeling sick himself, detours past the car yard on his way home from school and truly believes that the little grey car is shedding tears at the prospect of not being his – what a partnership – what excitement they could've shared ... When Abel gets home there's a phone call from Sergio's wife, Clara, she'll take over her husband's rounds until he recovers; as Abel conveys this thrilling development to Granny Annie dark clouds filter across her eyes: *Clara?!* Abel will work with the devil if it gets him the full deposit – and by Granny Annie's expression he may well have to – but all that's important is having that hot car in four weeks' time. Abel jumps into the yellow van as Clara pulls up in front of his house, overjoyed to make her acquaintance, not only is she the facilitator of the final steps towards his excitement machine, but she is a hot woman, in a black singlet top, black shorts and black sneakers, and a lot – like, really –

younger than her husband, and Abel starts to feel hot himself about this hot woman and his almost hands-on hot car, and is thrown back into his seat as Clara jams her foot down on the accelerator, her heavy tits flattening backwards with the force, Abel for some reason picturing Granny Annie's worried crinkles and he's not far wrong – be it the snapped glances from his new boss as he adjusts his balls – or Clara's deep-throated chuckle that puts him back eavesdropping on his mother and a boyfriend outside the lounge room … but not too much time for idle reflection, as on the first job – the two of them alone in an empty real-estate office – as soon as the cleaning is done, Abel reaches for the door handle to cart out the gear, but Clara's hand grabs his arm – vice like – and leads him back away from the door … Old Abel in the steamed-up car can still quote her next sentence, word for word: *Where do you want to do it, Abel, on the floor, the desk or in the bathroom up against the wall? … But why choose, ha?* Her chuckle so deep it vibrates in her tummy; she knows her super power over this young man. Abel freezes, all he can see is his mother shimmying as waves of the same deep-throated laughter roll like surf … *Why not all three, right?* … And so Abel finally understands the red-nosed driving instructor's spread-legged comments, it is a little scary as Clara not only lies down with spread legs but also sits up, leans back, stands, arches, rides and does a few more positions that Abel cannot immediately put into words, his brain exploding, Clara taking the lead, doing most of the heavy sex-work between them, and also supplying the spit and polish expertise at the finish, both boy and office glowing like lacquered furniture at the end – Sergio would've been proud. Over the next few weeks the balance of power shifts and Abel is called on to share the muscle work during their mad sex-romps, so that he's again thankful for his four days rest each week ... There is tenderness as well: Clara has started calling Abel *my bonus*; *So young – no shagger's back to worry about,* she often marvels out loud, the only downside being Granny Annie's exhausted look as she now waits up for him most nights, reminding Abel over and over what a good man Sergio is, how kind it was of him to employ young, inexperienced Abel, and how we should all do our best to pray for a speedy recovery and not dream of doing anything ever to hurt him. During one of his crawling under the house expeditions, Abel hears Granny Annie lament on the phone that from what she knows of Clara's reputation, it will be a miracle if Abel survives until Sergio recovers ... But he not only survives, he flourishes; four weeks later, when Sergio returns to work – which actually coincides with the day that Abel takes delivery of his little excitement machine – two things have changed: first, Sergio doesn't need to pick him up any longer, as Abel is more than delighted – ecstatic, in fact – to zoom around town in his hot little car and meet Sergio at the job; the second is that Abel learns a lesson that will stand him in good stead for the rest of his life. Women love sex if you well know how to present it; Clara's parting comment was *Abel, mate, your parents knew what they were doing when they gave you this name ...* as she hooked her arm around his neck for a long parting kiss ... *If I was rating you like a restaurant, I'd be crazy not to give you three dicks: one for erudition, one for performance and one for durability* … Ultimately, it was no different than getting his drivers licence: in this skill, too, he'd kind of practised for two years beforehand, but now, *ahhh*, finally official shagging accreditation. And yes, old Abel reflects now in the car, Granny Annie had a valid point, of not hurting a good man like Sergio, but what else could young Abel have done? He had merely been propelled towards Clara's jet bumper on the playfield and by the time the solenoid jolted into the round rubber skirt to kick him away, the four weeks had come and gone.

DING DING DING WOOOOP WOOOOP WAAK WAAK OWOWOWOWOW … Bouncing around on the playfield, there's no way – no matter what Abel is doing, no matter where he is, in or out of steam and fog, young or old – that he cannot think of Sir George-of-the-Jungle without grinning like a fool, even though for many, many years that memory is coupled with the pain in his chest of that twisted, burned-out hulk of a wheelchair and the two gaping skeletons … Roma, true to form, with corner smile, is teasing old Abel and has flipped the ball back to well before he got the car, and the white-clad nurse – if only he could acknowledge her – hovering over him nods, it's her understanding that this is the way for old Abel to eventually give a full account of himself. Abel is living with Granny Annie, going to the new school, being quiet and withdrawn: Abel has no friends. His boyhood best mate has been left behind in his old school, and since Mary got pregnant it's been all too awkward; having a fist fight now over his sister seems an impossibly remote option – did Dad punch Bernie out? Estrangement is easier – but anyway, the best mate problem is now a hundred miles away so it isn't in Abel's face and he tries not to think about it. He spends three nights a week working with Sergio and the rest of the nights and weekends either hangs out in town, or helps Granny Annie around the house and garden, or else goes bike riding; *I've just got to stick it out till I can leave school and make my own life*, he tells himself … Being a country boy Abel grew up on his bike so he brought it with him when he 'temporarily' moved to Granny Annie's place, and he now rides it along the cliff tops overlooking the ocean, and as old Abel sits in his foggy car he can feel the sun burning his back through the cotton shirt, feel the energy churn its way down his pumping body and the whiff of the clear cold breeze right up his nostrils makes his ears stand up and his eyes water. Every time he rides these cliff-top edges, he thinks of his yellow monster truck and Bernie going over head first – bounce, crash, slam, bang – much louder than a pinball cacophony … Abel rides up the steep incline, standing, leaning his weight on the handlebar and grinding the pedals, when he hears – or thinks he hears – a weak cry of *help* over the side. Abel stops and listens – distant crashing of waves below but nothing else – but he's sure he heard something, so he puts down the bike and crawls on his stomach to the edge of the cliff and looks over. And he is right, a few feet down, hanging onto shrubs, feet dangling in cold salty air, is a fat boy about Abel's age. *You okay, mate?* Stupid question … *HELP … HELP … HELP*, the boy cries, squinting to look up at his would-be saviour. Abel sees the smashed bike on the rocks below, majestically drawn into the incoming tide, he jumps up but sees no traffic or people coming either way. *Hang on*, he yells, stands, looks over the edge again, *It's a sheer drop*; he weighs up the dangerously steep decline, small shrubs rooted in rock outcrops, below his foot a small tree growing perpendicular to the cliff top; decision made, he takes off his pants and shirt, double knots them together then uses his belt to strap them around the tree trunk and dangle the clothes over the side like an awkward rope in a prison escape movie, then lies flat on his stomach with head over the edge: *Can you reach it?* – *I can't*, the boy yells back, but he's frozen stiff, hanging for dear life to the scrawny tree, his feet balancing on a loose, brown rock ... *I'm coming down*; Abel turns on his stomach, crawls backwards, hanging on to his dangling pants, drops his legs over the edge and feels his way to the first small tree, his sneakers making precarious contact, and he bounces on the trunk. *It all seems reasonably solid – HELP! I CAN'T HANG ON MUCH LONGER,* the boy whimpers. Abel bends his knees and gingerly lowers his body, his hands running down the full length of his hanging jeans, now virtually eye to eye with the boy; Abel reaches out: *Put one foot on that brown rock*, he nods down stiffly, *grip my hand and swing over ...* the boy shoots fearful glances ... *Come on, mate, I can't hang here all day* ... Even now, in the car, the nervous excitement builds like steam, but at the time, hanging off that cliff top, young Abel feels only fierce concentration; while the boy's terrified eyes are fixed on his rescuer, he reaches across, grabs the outstretched hand, uses the wobbly rock as a stepping stone, swings over to Abel's tree; the tree trembles with the weight of the boy's white-knuckled grip, and roots start to spring out one-by-one from their rock … *It's coming out … help!* … Abel head-butts and pushes the fat boy's arse up the incline; the boy, whimpering, shimmies up the clothes rope, hand over hand, and just before reaching safety, he unleashes a thundering fart right into his rescuer's face, and both boys yell, the fat boy with relief after he disappears over the top, and Abel with disgust at the in-his-face miasma, until finally, still spluttering, Abel heaves himself over the rocky edge and they lie side by side, exhausted, faces pressed into grass, trying to catch their breaths … Abel surveys the damage, his t-shirt and jocks a mess of dirt and mud and his shirt is ripped; Abel sticks his hand through the hole and wiggles his fingers: *Wouldn't have held together much longer* … The boy, still breathing hard, also sits up, cleaner and in better shape than his salvager: *George McCullum*, he extends his hand, still wheezing, *Thanks, I couldn't have held on much longer. I think you saved my life.… Sorry about … you know …* They stand up and shake. *I'm Abel Marvin … you okay?* The boy, George, still struggles to catch his breath, searches his pocket and stuffs an inhaler into his mouth, pumps twice … *Chronic asthma … when I'm stressed, or excited … like hanging off a cliff face.* Old Abel leans back in the car and cackles to himself, *He'd better not have a session with Clara, he'd never stop wheezing* … Standing, the boy is shorter than Abel, heavy set, and has freckles, blue eyes and tight curly blond hair … *Pushed me over the edge*, he squeezes out between breaths, *a bloody car flew around the corner and nearly collected me* … He and Abel look over the edge, the boy's bike serenely floating out with the tide … *I guess I'm walking back home – it's mostly downhill ... I can give you a dink ...* George's parents nominate Abel for a Bravery Award and old Abel's chest still swells as he sees himself standing up on the stage of the town hall, wearing his only formal shirt and tie, receiving his framed certificate under glass from the police chief. But the recollection is dampened by the attendance of his father, who's no longer his father, his mother who's no longer his mother, and Rose, who looks sickly guilty over Mary's absence. At the following reception, his father's eyes are cloudy, as if stuck in the recollection of his only son's vision of his wife having it off with Bernie, who then tumbles and squashes Ginger the kitten; his mother's smile is that of a window mannequin, fixed and unrelenting; Rose's bottom lip quivers and Granny Annie clasps one hand with the other so as not to slap her son's face ... all heaped and covered by lots of pride-in-Abel platitudes, best-of-luck wishes, but then at the first opportunity they are gone.

Not even one – *give yourself a pat on the back, mate –* from Dad.

Not even one – *come back home to live with us, we miss you –* from Mum.

Not even one – *you did nothing wrong, Ali, Mary fucked up –* from Rose.

Old Abel gently turns young Abel around towards the applauding and waving 'new family': George, Roma, George's parents and Roma's father, the chief of police, Frank, as they pull the award-winning boy into their midst ... *Don't look back, Abel, just don't look back! ...* Yet another stark vision to muddy the clear waters when all those years later Abel gets that irresistible offer to change sides from *Abel* to *Jackson* and walk away forever from his family's turned backs into a bright and promising future.

The Bravery Award is the least of Abel's dividends from that cliff rescue; George and Abel are the same age so the best part is that George asks Abel over for tea. Abel loves going to the McCullums; George's mother makes spaghetti (called pasta), potato dumplings (called gnocchi), spiked with hot sauces and spices, nothing like the bland fare of Granny Annie … George's father runs the local newspaper, *The Prospector*, so apart from the exotic food, mealtime is a happening place as they argue about cutting down trees, old trees, new trees, greenies, living-wages, minimum wages, the poverty line, or talk about books and films and stuff like that … *You've got to read* Dune, *Abel, the most amazing sci-fi novel ever – no, no* … In the Heat of the Night … *Couldn't put it down and they're making a film from it – hey, Abel, have you seen* Doctor Zhivago, *what a masterpiece!* – The Spy Who Came in from the Cold? *Amazing flick, so tense – That's the John le Carré book, right? – We're doing* Virginia Woolf *in school – That's a bit ambitious – The Albee play, not the writer – I'm in it – What as, Martha or Honey?* … Laughter all around, and since Abel doesn't understand much of it, he just eats more spaghetti doused with chilli … But the best part of dinner is the dinner table setting: *underplates* for every dish – Abel has never seen underplates before – funny, as though they're about to place the soup, pasta and meat dishes on the sea and serenely float them off … bye, bye, dinner setting, have a good trip … but even better are the cloth napkins in their ceramic ring holders, Abel's sky blue with tiny white sailboats ... Then the best part of all, after tea George takes Abel to his room and shows him books and magazines and newspapers from all over the world, he plays music called jazz, and goes all dreamy-eyed and nods his head slowly and says: *Listen, listen to this piano, Abel ...* especially that blasting tune without words, *Sing, Sing, Sing ...* Abel smiles at the same place each time and for sure George holds up one finger and says on cue ... *Listen, listen, Jess Stacy, isn't he something? ... Jess Stacy, yeah!* ... George also has a terrific comic book collection; it takes up half the wall in his room, some really old, worn-out comics whose pages he turns with care – Superman, Captain Marvel, Batman – but also some others that Abel has never heard of, funny ones like Katzenjammer Kids and Ginger Meggs ... George and Abel sit on the floor, leaning against the bed, laughing at the shenanigans, then George starts lending him comics to take home, armfuls of them; Abel loves reading them much better than books or newspapers, because it's as though the characters in the pictures look at him and are talking to him in the balloons over their heads, and quite often he speaks back, commenting on their adventures, thinking of these animated people as George's private gang, so they become his friends as well ... George takes his new hero-friend on a tour of his dad's newspaper office, the two boys stepping out of the lift into a hectic news world, a huge room, with desks, chairs, dividing screens, people shouting, running, laughing, carrying papers and conversing in corners, typewriters banging like machine guns; George steers Abel to his cubicle, and sits him down on his own swivel chair in front of the typewriter, the desk a mess of papers and cut-outs and inks and glues of every colour and bowls of chocolates to give Granny Annie's sweeties a run for their money ... After the visit Abel follows his new friend's cadet career in *The Prospector*, he reads George's articles on 'The Aussie Tarzan', a five-year-old boy lost in the bush and living wild ... 'Down Goes Our Heritage', charming old buildings torn down to make room for no-personality office blocks ... 'Sustenance', how much can a family of five live on? ... but the most important headline of all – 'SAVING THIS BUDDING JOURNO'S HIDE' the bold, page-one account with pictures of how Abel Jackson Marvin saved George McCullum; reading the story out loud to Granny Annie, Abel has to admit that he doesn't recall quite that amount of danger, tension, savage seas, steep decline, sharp brittle rocks or matchstick trees yanking out of the cliff face, nor does he remember being as calm as Superman and as decisive as Batman, and certainly – Abel is positive – he did not stand on top of the cliff edge and yell *SHAZAM – struck by a magic lightning bolt and transformed into Captain Marvel then swooped down to save young McCullum in distress – Newspapers have their own language, their way of saying things*, Granny Annie explains, *no wonder they call George the fantasy writer* – but she cuts out the article, has it framed under glass and Abel uses it in later years to great effect at job interviews ... But the best, best part – Abel salivates with delight in the car – even better than the food, underplates and comics – is George's girlfriend, Roma ... if everything about

George's world is a whirlwind to young Abel, then his girlfriend, Roma, is the eye of the storm ... On their first meeting, she places her hands on her hips and pronounces for all to hear: *So you are the culprit who saved George-of-the-Jungle's life?* While Abel is stuck for words, grinning George introduces them, he then leans over and giggles something into Roma's ear; *You didn't? ...* Roma's mouth drops open ... *in his face? ...* She then turns to Abel: *I would've thrown him right back, Mr Marvin ... Next time you see this rascal dangling from a tree, I'd look the other way – Fart or not,* thinks Abel, *one I flipped over the edge on the stairs, and one I pulled back up from the cliffs, the randomness of kickers and slingshots, yet still there's an elegant balance.* But it much more than merely balances out – saving George's life shows a mega profit; Roma touches his cheeks with both hands, sending sizzles down his spine; *Thank you, Abel,* she heaves, her eyes pools of black tears, *I don't know what I'd do without my George ...* and she leans forward and kisses Abel on the lips.

Pull the pin, hear the ping, silver ball bounce and ding ... The first few times that Abel and Roma meet, Abel is way too shy to say one word to her. Looking at Roma is like staring directly into the sun; after a couple of seconds his retinas threaten to melt and he has to lower his eyes, so Abel begins donning sunglasses whenever Roma is around – everyone thinks he's trying hard for *cool,* but it's no more than a handy sunscreen ... A week after the rescue, long before the award, George and Abel go after dinner to Wing Hong's amusement arcade in High Street to play pinball; Roma walks in and without a word she and George hug and kiss passionately like in the movies, right in front of everyone, she then makes her hands-on-hips announcement, touches and kisses Abel, and even now in the steamy car, more than fifty years later, Abel's breathing becomes laboured watching the scene on the wide, 3D screen in his face, furious at the name calling from behind him, trying to distract him from re-living that dumbfounding, glorious pivotal moment ... *Roma* ... *Roma* ... *Roma* ... he chants and pounds the steering wheel. Roma could be no greater contrast to whizzing George: slim, with thick, long black hair parted in the middle, then swept around to one side, coiled like springy rope onto her chest; she loves to laugh – at everything – and is just over six feet tall, same height as Abel, and taller than George. Big black eyes – extend on demand – and a laugh that sucks him in ... When she joined them for dinner Abel looked down at his plate and smiled the whole time, sometimes neglecting his food and losing track of political discussions. After Roma mentioned they were doing *Who's Afraid of Virginia Woolf?* in school, Abel went to the library – burning with embarrassment – borrowed the play and visualised Roma as Honey (she'd be one hell of an actress to play that scatterbrained, mousy wife who makes those dim-witted comments). But old Abel is drawn back again to that kiss; when she touches and kisses him on the lips, Abel understands why George is always short of breath: for a long moment Abel's body is too stunned to suck in air, and from that first touch Abel becomes fascinated with this girl's hands, the long, slim olive wrists and lustrous fingers, as if they were invincible. Old Abel is propelled back to when as a young tyke Dad had taken

him to the circus for the first time. Afterwards, outside
the tent, on the tray of a flatbed truck stood a tall woman
with long black hair who spread her fingers and promised
that her hands could heal, bless, bring luck and babies –
just one adorned, lengthy touch, for a small fee, and all
wishes would eventuate – she linked eyes with the young
boy, slowly rotated her magic hands and they glowed
as though indeed blessed by the supernatural ... And
as though locked in to that imagery, Roma sets about
proving her hands' invincibility, soon after she touches
and kisses Abel, she wipes away her tear tracks, and plays
at the next pinball machine, singing softly: *Pull the pin,
hear the ping, silver ball bounce and ding – What would a
girl know about pinball?* Abel smirks – what indeed? He
stands stupefied as she pulls back the pin, shoots out the
steel balls then rams the flippers, ricocheting the balls
back into action – points racking up on the back glass
– *These poor, rundown machines, they need a service, a good
spit and polish,* she laments, then cackles, *think I'll get Dad
to issue a summons to have them spruced up ... Wanna game,
Abel?* She licks her lips, hikes her eyebrows and flips
the flippers with a tease – *You're being hustled, my friend,*
George laughs, *The lady has a cellar full of pinnies at home –
has been pinging those silver balls since she could stick her nose
above the playfield.* George hugs his girlfriend sideways
and kisses her cheek: *Go on, Dame Romani, sing us your
mantra.* Letting go of the flippers Roma straightens up
and with trademark corner grin sings: *Pull the pin, hear
the ping, silver ball bounce and ding. Keep control, flip it
back to spin and thwack. Toss it, flick it, swirl and gain. But
never, never let that ball drain.*

When Roma has dinner with them at George's house, afterwards the three of them go to her dad's cellar to play his pinnies; with Roma's police chief dad too busy to play, the cellar becomes the trio's private clubhouse. Roma, an only child, the cellar being her cloistered space, is thrilled with the company. She shows the boys how to remove the wired glass slats from outside the cellar window so they can slide in and jump down without going through the house. In the brightly lit cellar rows of spotlights aim down at the banks of pinball machines, the seven-year-old Roma stares down from a framed photo, her head barely above the pinnie she's embracing, 'Tommy – The Pinball Wizard' soundtrack blasts at full volume, they join in a chorus of friendship, singing and playing the machines old and new – eating fish and chips, drinking beer, smoking and laughing a lot, all the time … all, all the time … *Hey Abel, try Buckaroo, spin roto target and bucking horse that kicks butt when the jet bumpers light up … no, no way, try Paradise, get a load of the hula dancer swinging her hips … Lucky Strike is the coolest, the bowling game …* Roma doles nicknames like knighthoods to the boys, making capes from cut-up sheets … for Abel, a black cape with a crude red drawing of Mandrake, top hat and cane, holding out a hypnotising hand with spread fingers … for George, white cape, green trees and swinging monkeys … for herself, the Romani flag, blue and green cape with the large red spoke wheel in the middle. *Arise, Sir George-of-the-Jungle … Arise, Sir Marvin-the-Magician,* she says, positioning their capes, tapping them on each shoulder, then she cloaks herself, dons a red jockey hat and taps herself left and right: *Arise, Dame Gypsy-of-the-Romani,* then takes lots and lots of Polaroids – click, eject, peel off, laugh – and so they become the Knights and Dame of the Pinnie Basement Gang; *Dame Roma-the-Firecracker*, Abel secretly names her ... After Abel married Pamsy, and George and Roma were married as well, Abel would still be invited to the occasional dinner at George's parents' house; he'd tell Pamsy that he was working late at the warehouse, then drive over and have a great meal and lots of laughs reminiscing about the old *pinnie gang* days; sometimes also, after work, he'd drive to Roma's giant, dark house, remove the window slats and slip into the basement, nod to the photo of seven-year-old Roma, don his Mandrake cape, and play the pinnies till late, his heart always skipping a beat as he turned off the bank of overhead spotlights and the noisy, bright amusement world disappeared into darkness ... Abel in the car struggles to twist and turn his head away from the wide screen, he wants to stop there, let the ball drain, those next few scenes difficult enough living through once, twice is too much, even in a swirling steam-fog, but the screen thunders through the mist: *Can't quit yet, mate – have you given a full account of yourself?* Old Abel is on the verge of recognition, he knows that white-clad nurse slipping in and out of his vision but can't quite identify her, even her voice is now becoming more familiar: *Who is she and why is she harassing me now? ... Piss off!* Abel wants to be left alone to enjoy those happy years when George and Roma now work at *The Prospector*, Roma in the office and George as reporter, but it all zooms past too fast – *slow down, slow down, these good times are never to be repeated* – he can do nothing about it, this meal at

George's parents' place is destined to be the saddest, and the last, Abel arrives neat and clean-shaven, walking in the door with his usual smiling *g'day* and a bunch of flowers for George's mum that he can still smell in the car – Abel knows instantly that something is wrong … dour expressions ricochet off the walls decapitating the bunch of flowers, chairs are dragged from the table across the wooden floor, no one even acknowledges the flowers … George looks up with teary eyes … *What happened, mate?* Abel scans the row of dejected faces – *Haven't you seen the news? – No, been at work till now* … A searching look from George, almost insulted, *Work is no excuse*, it says; Roma's face is tense, centring on George … *Someone has died, no doubt*, Abel sums up and he isn't far wrong; George's father shakes his head: *It'll be alright, George, the country … the people will never let this happen*; Abel still looks around for clues; George's mother rises slowly, and begins dishing out the veal pieces in the brown lemon sauce that Abel loves, Abel looks at Roma – *Our Prime Minister has been sacked* … Abel shifts his focus to George – *A fucking colony … that's what we are. No more than a fucking British colony – Gough Whitlam?* Abel catches on finally, *Who sacked him? – Kerr … The Governor-General. That fat drunk … He'll never get away with it*, George pounds the table, *Demonstrations, marches, blood will flow in the streets* – George foretells – George's father chimes in: *Gough said, 'God save the Queen, but nothing will save the Governor-General' – We'll all see to that*, George adds, face swollen with anger. With addled expression Abel runs his fingers through his backwards swept hair, unsure if he understands the crisis correctly … all this fuss over a political sacking? Surely an overreaction. George's mother's hand shakes as she serves Abel the brown-sauced potatoes, she looks up, her eyes are deep pools remembering how Abel saved her only son. George is choked up, he can't eat – a first. He gets up and goes into his old room in his parents' house. After a moment's silence, Roma makes a move to follow, but Abel, surprising himself, holds out his 'Mandrake' hand fingers spread, and follows his friend. Abel hasn't been in George's boyhood room for years, but little has changed. Stacks of comics on the shelf, colourful old jazz albums piled up. Except that they are no longer boys. George the man is sitting on the floor, leaning back on his old bed, holding his head with both hands. Abel picks up an old *MAD* magazine, with the goofy Alfred E Neuman on the cover, the boy with the misaligned eyes and gap-toothed smile, and he reads out the perennial motto: *What, me worry?* George scans Abel's face to the magazine and Abel is smacked with the worst of all scenarios: George – the joker, the fantasy boy journo – is mute. Barely a few days later, on the nightly news Abel watches at home with Pamsy, sees the demonstration … talk about overreaction, many thousands of people rallying in Melbourne, workers, students and assorted multitudes, defenders of the democratic process. But the highlight, replayed many times, the Buckaroo pinball back glass firing to life – the panicked policeman's horse backing up, tottering, back leg shooting out, kicking the young journalist George McCullum in the forehead – Abel's hand whacks down on Pamsy's arm – does he scream out? He can't remember. George falls in slow motion, the back of his head hits a metal barrier, the camera zooms in on the iron smeared with blood – Abel asks himself all those years later: *If you save someone's life, are you responsible for them forever?* And without turning his head old Abel can feel the white-clad nurse behind him pondering the very same dilemma.

Roma and George disappear. Abel drops in on Chief Frank, but is told Roma and George are in a hospital and would prefer complete privacy. Then, in answer to his heartbroken look, Chief Frank adds: *Give them time, Abel, they said to tell you that they love you, but please give them time. – They said?* Abel's eyes inquire. Slight shrug from Chief Frank. Abel checks the newspapers, flips through TV news channels, draws blanks. Roma and George seem to have fallen off the edge of the earth. He wakes nights with that repeated vision of kick and fall. Glistening blood on metal. For weeks he rings George's mother … *Any news? … Where are they?* After a few months Abel breaks down; he goes to see George's mother. They sit quietly on opposite couches, no merrymaking, no din and no pasta with chilli … *George and Roma are the best friends I ever had, I can't rest, can't concentrate at work.* George's mother, stooped over, nods slowly, her face dry, so deeply furrowed with sadness that Abel can't bring himself to ask directly about George. *Roma knows, Abel, she loves you just as much. I'll try.* Now Abel is worried even more. *Roma knows? … What about George?* A couple of weeks later George's mother rings Abel at work and tells him that Roma can meet him that night at her father's place. Abel leaves work early, picks up the blue tray full of Glad-Wrapped sweeties from Granny Annie's, drives to Roma's father's house, removes the window slats and slips into the basement, flicking on the bank of overhead spotlights that explode into a sea of white waves. CLANG CLANG CLANG DING DING DING WOOOOP WOOOOP WAAK WAAK OWOWOWOWOW ... Old Abel's fingers tingle with the sensitive pressure he applies to the flippers, trying to stop the slippery silver ball from scooting past and draining. After midnight, with Abel on the verge of giving up, Roma slides through the basement window and clunks herself down ... but no ... wait, this can't be Roma, because that girl would normally flick her coiled hair and land on tippy-toes like an Olympic gymnast, then curtsey to accompanying applause ... but not on this night: Roma crashes down; dragging a bottle of vodka behind her, she totters to Buckaroo, flicks the switch and the pinnie explodes into bursts of light and sound; she plunks the dusty red jockey's hat on her head and shoots off the silver ball into the playfield; finally raising her eyes, tears well up from the silent deep, glisten down her cheeks, and she whimpers: *There's no plan, is there, Abel? Mum died when I was born, Dad is always busy ... Then I found George ... George, my future, my lover and my brother ... The McCullums are my family, Abel* – she punishes the flippers, the ball hits the jet bumpers CLANG CLANG CLANG they light up and the horse bucks and kicks the clown's backside, sending him tumbling and rolling – Roma's arched body shudders – *and now George ... George ... What control do we have, Abel? Bugger all!* DING DING DING WOOOOP WOOOOP – *a few flipper jabs* – WAAK WAAK –

a tilt here and there, what? ... What? ... What else? Nothing. The ball just rolls wherever – George *kicked to hell –* OWOWOWOWOW *– Where is this fucking ball bearing going to bounce off next, Abel? ... Maybe just let it drain and it's all ... all ...* Abel knows all about losing and gaining new family – fuck, he could write a thesis on it; he encircles Roma in his arms, hugs her with all his strength, and as she surrenders he eases them down onto the floor beneath her framed seven-year-old self ... *He doesn't recognise me,* Roma babbles, *doesn't know who I am ...* – the words block her throat, she chokes – *he ... he ... can't speak ... can't walk ... just sits and nods ... George just sits and nods ...* Finally the crying finds its way out, Roma convulses in Abel's embrace, the skin under his shirt sizzles with her closeness; he waits until she calms a little then eases her back against the wall ... *Abel* – she heaves, her gleaming black eyes bore into him from five inches away – *they've suspended George's treatment ... we'll never have babies now ... even if I could ... get him to ... to ...* She bursts into tears; Abel holds her closely until she stops; sniffing, Roma wipes her face with her sleeve and drags the bottle over, uncorks it, takes a long swig and offers it to Abel, he takes a drink as well, steadies Roma, gently lets go ... *I'll just be a tick ...* He holds her eyes like Mandrake, extended hand, spread fingers, brings over the plastic-covered plate – *Granny Annie says that a plate full of sweeties can help balance out the nasties of life* – he looks down, shrugs foolishly, offering Roma the tray; she takes a pink meringue and bites into it, Abel takes a white one, Roma's T-shirt slips off one pointed, fragile shoulder, more tears drip down, the edges of her meringue are soon wet – *George is in a wheelchair … he … he slumps to one side … he … he doesn't know who I am … Abel, he doesn't know …* Roma swigs another drink with a mouthful of meringue, the bottle neck now covered with pink crumbs; Abel takes a sip, more for the crumbs than the vodka, the clear liquid all the sweeter now. The room explodes with the stark brightness of the surreal, as Roma jerks up … thoughts race across her forehead like winning scores scrolling the pinnie's back glass – the old Roma, nimble and full of spring, flicks on the 'Tommy' soundtrack, grabs the three capes – as though following a prompter – strips off Abel's shirt, her extended, jumping eyes and trembling hands all over his face, chest and back, stroking, lighting fires and engaging currents, now murmuring, *George … George …* She ties the Mandrake magical cape around Abel's naked shoulders, in the same blinded, automaton action, throws off her striped sailor's top, kicks off her silver-toed boots and strips off her jeans, tugging Abel's clothes as though they are an unacceptable barrier … Abel undresses in a dream; Roma drapes herself in the Romani flag cape, spreads George's jungle cape on the hard cement floor, dons the jockey hat and lies down, dragging Abel on top of her: *George, George … Make love to me, please … I need a baby to love and to hold or I'll die … you saved a life once, Sir Marvin-the-Magician, please save Dame Gypsy-of-the-Romani now … I need a baby for George … for George … please …* Roma's kisses brand his lips – *You know what*, she whispers in his ear, *maybe this is one shot I can control* – she runs her fingers through his hair, strokes his cheeks ever so gently, the sizzle working its way down and Abel falls back onto the faith-healing woman outside the circus tent, swivelling those lustrous hands, locking eyes, whispering seductively to young Abel: *One adorned touch and I can promise you luck, health and babies ... babies ...*

Back in the car Abel feels an urgent need to escape. *Abel ... Abel ... Abel ...* The name calling from behind has intensified; though the female voice dissolves into the mist, the white-clad nurse never tires of her mantra: *Have you given a full account of yourself?* Her voice echoes in a silent, hangar-like auditorium. But the steamy womb is cosy, he ignores the name calling and lies back, breathes in and out the world of vapour, reliving the time when years later, he takes Pamsy to see the movie *Tommy* – that kid who can't control anything in his life *except* for the bouncing silver balls – featuring the Buckaroo pinnie, the screaming music, scoring bells, clicking metal balls, banging plastic flippers on the playfield – then the horse bucks and kicks the clown on the back glass and a wheelchair parade of damaged, nodding people lean over, hoping for a miracle cure in the Marilyn Monroe cathedral – he sees crippled George among them, slumping to one side, nodding, wheelchair pushed by white-knuckle grip, hypnotised Roma – it deposits Abel back onto that basement floor making blind love to Roma over and over; Abel tries to stand in the dark theatre and almost passes out thinking of *those hands ... hands that gave life and babies – when she touched me, she gave some of herself ...* remembering what she whispered in his ear: *Maybe this is one shot I can control.* Later in the noisy foyer a soothing Pam reminds Abel: *Roma was right, a lot of good came out of that night, Abel, be proud of it*. But – no, NO-O-O-O – don't think about that now – remember – concentrate, press hands to temples, return to well before the bucking horses, the metal and blood, replay the couple's golden period, George and Roma are in university, coming home only on some weekends and during holidays. They are unofficially engaged, but hey, they've been in that state since the day they met in high school. George still contributes the occasional article to *The Prospector* that Abel reads at work, sometimes several times a day. *TWO COUNTRY BUMPKINS IN THE BIG SMOKE … TO BE OR NOT TO BE A CITY DWELLER* – here again the young journalist uses his fantasy licence: picture of George donning a cloak and feather bonnet, a city-bound Hamlet, wandering Melbourne's graffiti-clad lanes, pondering that question out loud. On the occasions the old pinnie gang meet for dinner at the McCullums', or in the pub for a drink, or spend a raucous evening banging steel balls all over the place, Roma and George are probably in the happiest state that Abel has seen them since they met. And their happiness rubs off, it travels around the playfields, and CLANG DING WOOPS drains out of the machine and onto Abel's hands clutching the flippers. It infuses his body like a summer blush and his face just about tires from smiling all night at those two devils' shenanigans … Abel now is a fully-fledged man, still living with Granny Annie; he's finally landed full-time employment, his first job – that will also be his last – at Product Line Warehouse; he works for minimum wage doing shit jobs, well you've got to start somewhere … Abel surrounded by a fortress of boxes filled with gadgets, slits the cartons open, takes out the video recorders, cordless house phones, tape recorders, child monitors, et cetera, removes the *NOT TO BE SOLD OUTSIDE THE USA* label, and the smaller *Made in China* stickers, and attaches *MADE IN AUSTRALIA* stickers with strips of Aussie flags, which he does box by box, hour by hour, day after day, except for the times he gets the factory lunches from the mobile lunch van in front of the warehouse, or when he collects rubbish from the unpacking, sorting, picking and repacking stations around the warehouse – a hangar-like structure as big as two football fields – but it's due to this shit-kicking activity that Abel gets his first raise in pay and a trophy, as one morning he blissfully walks into the front office to clean out the bins in the middle of an armed hold-up, the two stocking-masked men with the sawn-off shotguns freeze as Abel trumpets through the door pulling his clunky garbage cage on wheels: *This is it, girls and boys, give it all up to Abel.* A moment's stand-off while the two masked men stare at Abel, rotating their shotguns in slow motion directly at his chest. As Abel absorbs the shotguns pointed at him, the trembling staff lying on the carpet with hands behind heads and only the senior bookkeeper emptying out the giant black safe, he makes a swift about-turn and runs back screaming that they are being held up – a miracle that they don't shoot him – but thanks to Abel's panic the robbers make a hasty escape with the meagre petty-cash box – this heroism, for the second time in Abel's life, reaffirms to all that the first sea-cliff rescue wasn't a fluke, and apart from a decent pay rise, it has a sizable side-effect of endearing Abel to the rank and file workers who start teaching young Abel Vietnamese on the job, since the owners, and all the staff except Abel, are Vietnamese, well, he hasn't really learned much of the sing-song language except for words he can repeat only to the men, because they are not for polite society; the upside is they are extremely friendly and jolly and his daily lunch order task is fairly light as most of the employees bring their own food to work heating it up in the kitchen, and talk about 'bonus' – as Clara had taught him – the bonus here is Anita … Both Abels go mushy at the thought of the married mother of two who looks no older than a teenager and works in a packing station handling imported textiles; when Anita walks back to her work station after lunch, past his pyramid of boxes, her black, almond-shaped eyes bounce one solid gaze off Abel, but that is more than enough to deliver the message – that one sharp stab brings to mind all of Abel's Vietnamese swear words – *Don't go there,* old Abel whispers through the fog into young Abel's ear, though he knows that ear is deaf when it comes to Anita – and on the face of it, there's no need for caution, because Anita is out of bounds, her husband, also teenage-looking, drops her off and picks her up in front of the warehouse every day and everyone knows it … Except for that one week when his car has broken down and Anita has to commute by bus, and on the second day, on her post lunchtime walk back to her work station, she whips him with a radioactive glance, Abel knocks over his drink on top of the cardboard shoebox, and the painted Aussie flags drip patriotism. After work he drives past the bus stop in his excitement machine – surely so much more exhilarating than her husband's rusty old Holden – Anita, waiting there, bathes his car from front bumper to back fender with a glance and young and old Abel inside feel as though the car has now been baptised for … well, anything, but of course, too many other Product Line staff stand at the bus stop, so Abel follows the bus at a respectable distance … Anita at the back of the bus re-bathes the car before sitting down … After many stops Anita gets off the bus, walks without looking back and, when the bus is out of sight, slips into the Mini as though she was made-to-fit that bucket front seat, they drive to the beach and silently fuck standing up in a ladies' public toilet, Anita hanging from Abel like a nursing child – years later, this afternoon's delight comes to mind when Abel sees an ad for Mini Minors: *When you drive a Mini – you don't have to prove a thing* – but at the time, once Anita's husband starts picking her up again, one day the husband takes out a gun and shoots Anita and the manager of her section, right in the parking lot … She survives, but the manager dies and her husband goes to jail – Abel is informed by leery co-workers that Anita had a heated affair with her manager, who drove a state-of-the-art green and silver Ford Zephyr – Abel thanks his lucky stars that he could only afford a striped Mini, its attraction limited to a one-afternoon stand.

How easily his destination could have taken another turn – silver ball bouncing off a different bumper – Abel having nearly been shot in the Product Line car park relaxes back in the foggy car. He lifts his right leg to dashboard height and wiggles the naked toes; that foot is to blame – or be congratulated – for his lifetime job at the warehouse, his brief encounter with Anita and ultimately for meeting his life-long wife, Pamsy ... At the same time as being filled with dread at another life that may have so easily been his lot, Abel is also smug and snug in the recollection of what it was like to be totally drunk, alcohol, lots of it, having dowsed his virility, lowered his testosterone level and replaced it with a dreamy sleepiness of wafting alongside the creek on his own, heading nowhere, and being in no hurry to get there ... After leaving school it had been confirmed – with minimum phone argy-bargy – that he'd moved permanently to Granny Annie's house (for the time being). Abel was conflicted about the news – he'd never again be close pals with his dad – although that secure warmness was fading so fast he had to work hard to remind himself of the snugness of Dad pulling him closer in the sleeping bags – had it ever existed? The sunshine-drenched cone-shaped bush cathedral, key hidden under log, never to be retrieved again. It also meant he no longer had a mother, but the worst of all was he'd lost his two sisters. He wished for the days when the little squirrels hugged him at school then bounced off his belly in bed, but mostly he wished he could be near them to help them grow up. Indeed, the 5×M+D photograph was retreating so far that he occasionally examined the picture, sure it was fading under the glass. Had he really scratched them that night? But the plus side was the warm hug he got from Roma and the slap on the back from George when he told them the news of his permanent tenure at Granny Annie's – *We've got you now forever, Sir Marvin-the-Magician*, Roma kissed his cheek, *Yeah, for better or worse,* George added, *We're just too flat out to go looking for another member for the pinnie gang.* George drew a square in the air and wrote: *Wanted urgently: pinnie playing gang member with cranky sense of humour, lanky Jimmy Stewart swept-back hair, hypnotic qualities and a knighthood …*

Abel unsuccessfully applies for several jobs, but one morning is lucky enough to land what he considers his dream job: an apprenticeship in the jewellery-making trade. Granny Annie had a boxful of intricate silver jewellery that her father, an adventurer, had brought back from South America. Abel had occasionally spread the silver cache out on a soft black cloth and picking up each piece had marvelled at the complex miniature soldering and finely strung wires that held them together … *Love to make some of these beauties,* he'd confided to his grandmother, never imagining that a job like that could ever be in the offing … But it was and after two interviews – and even though he lacked education and was well past the ideal apprentice age – the smiling boss congratulated him on getting this rare learning opportunity, so celebrating, drunken Abel kicks a can that sails into the dark creek waters – while both Abels, young and old – whoop at the daring approach Abel had taken to this interview. First he showed the framed article and photo of his heroism, inviting the boss to ring the McCullum family for a character reference, the future boss said that it wouldn't be necessary, then asked Abel if he had the patience to sit long hours tinkering with small delicate things – Abel whipped out from his wallet the old photo Granny Annie had taken of him sitting on the floor surrounded by a wooden-block city, made up of the tiniest to the largest blocks; Abel then went on to describe in great detail the many hours – hundreds, in fact – that he had spent as a youth patiently assembling these structures, sometimes not going to bed till very late, so obsessed in the logistics of joining so many different-size blocks to work together, to indeed, sparkle like a bejewelled city – he left out blasting that collection to smithereens with his best mate's shotgun – the prospective boss bemused but intrigued took him for a tour of the workshop, where three young men, with neat haircuts, all in white, monogrammed dustcoats, wore flip-up small magnifying glasses, worked on personal benches, each with a selection of tiny tools for grinding, soldering, magnifying, et cetera, and before each apprentice stood a row of diamonds from tiny sparkling to oh-my-God glittering beauties, and gemstones of all colours, lustrous amber, succulent ruby and layered jade plus fine gleaming silver wires. Abel saw his own reflection in the shiny jewellery and he felt a surge of confidence; he naturally belonged among those precious stones. Abel tenderly patted the fourth, empty workbench, and lovingly smoothed down the row of neatly laid-out tools, just waiting for him, then he turned to the man and said: *If you hire me you won't be sorry. I love building, striking, tiny things … perfect every time …* So he gets the job, but with one proviso: *We run a tight ship here, no drinking on the job, no coming in hungover – these tools are precious, these gems priceless. If you stuff up there's no going back, thousands of dollars down the drain.* Outside the establishment's front door, Abel grips one hand with the other in fierce congratulation and since he isn't starting until Wednesday, two days away, Abel goes to the nearest pub, orders a beer, and says, *Good job, Abel my boy, give yourself a pat on the back, mate* – patting himself he laughs, and others at the bar laugh with him, so he buys them all a round, boasting of the perfect job he's just landed, they drink and banter until it's dark and when Abel leaves the pub, stumbling about, rather than going back to face Granny Annie, he walks along the little creek outside the town, re-living his brave interview and congratulating himself for being a jewel among diamonds ... BANG CRASH BOOM ... Abel is knocked over on the narrow, grassy path, his right foot screaming with pain and his head lashed, he struggles to dig himself out from under the bike ... *Fucking drunken yobbo, swaying all over the path ... didn't you hear me yell ON YOUR RIGHT?* ... While the fuming man fiddles with his mangled bike, Abel blubbers an apology, the cursing cyclist shoulders his bike and marches out pack-mule-like, and Abel sits up, his foot throbbing like hell. Old Abel can still feel the cutting pain as young Abel limps up to the bank; it takes a while in his drunken state to convince someone to call a taxi which takes him to the nearest hospital ... The next day he's sent home to Granny Annie's in a cast – bones in his foot fractured – too embarrassed to ring the jewellers since the police report shows his embarrassingly high blood alcohol level; Abel simply doesn't show up to work that Wednesday, abandoning his dream of crowned, jewelled cities, then some weeks later, when his foot is better, again flashing his heroism article, he gets the job as the shit-kicker at Product Line Warehouse ... If he'd told Granny Annie about losing the job at the best and most respected jewellery store in town, one tray of sweeties wouldn't have been enough … way too many nasties. But, hey, old Abel comforts young Abel wiggling his foot, it didn't turn out so bad, did it? Maybe he just wasn't up to scratch, maybe just a lesser jewel for flipping Bernie down the stairs and betraying Sergio by fucking Clara. He'd just need to pull those plungers back and fire himself off to another, less sparkling, destiny – the playfield at the warehouse – but then, years later, the jet bumpers spring another surprise by flooding the highways and keeping him in another woman's bed for that one-night stand and a second – and last – offer of a better life.

Abel becomes official safety officer soon after starting work, in fact, surprisingly fast – just after the armed robbery – he's called into the boss's office where the man himself presents him with the title and a special grey dustcoat with his name and new rank embroidered on the pocket … He also receives an impressive raise, and all he really has to do to is sign a monthly certificate stating that he has inspected the huge warehouse, and found it to fit all civil, legal and union requirements, a document that someone else has already filled out, yet Abel always gets a kick seeing his name and new title printed on the document, alongside his signature … After the first few months Abel has a beer with George and boasts about this safety officer business, George rages, *That position is bullshit, an obvious scam*, claiming they are using Abel – the only non-Vietnamese person – and his Bravery Award as a patsy – if someone gets run over by a charging forklift or crushed by a collapsed, overstocked shelf, they will blame Abel; *Mate, you've got three choices*, George informs his friend, both Abels are immobile, this is a far cry from George's usual jolliness: *I can write an article in* The Prospector *and blow the scheme sky high, or you can go to the unions and they'll put a stop to it … or you can just quit …* But Abel does nothing, where would a lesser jewel like him find another job with such pay and prospects? But also, this new position has a perk that no one else knows about … the new safety officer is in charge of where to put many thousands of new cartons arriving weekly around the hangar-like building, and he decides to stack quite a few on the ceiling of the ladies' toilets, a space previously sitting empty. One day as he cleans the dust off the toilet ceiling behind the cartons, Abel's elbow breaks through the thin chipboard, as he goes into the toilet to clean the woodchip crumbs on the floor he looks up – since the toilet is brightly lit, the space over the roof is pitch dark – all he can see is a tiny paint crack and nothing beyond, and hence Abel Jackson Marvin now has his own private porn gallery. Every day just before knock off, a constant stream of girls of all ages go in and out of the toilets, and since no one ever checks up on Abel – in fact, as long as he signs his monthly safety statements on time, no one bothers him at all – Abel spends quite a bit of productive time lying flat on his stomach in the ceiling dust, right eye glued to the brightly lit female activity below: periods, pregnancies and masturbation fantasies … Of course, he soon has his favourites: the younger, unmarried women, many preparing for dates after work – strip down for a quick pee, change to going-out clothes, some even hold small mirrors inspecting that all is ship-shape below for that all-important date, the mirror giving Abel a bird's-eye view of the inner sanctum ... The very same hold-up bookkeeper is one of Abel's favourites, when she first started she used to masturbate to Paul Newman's glossy photograph pinned to the cubicle door, Paul's blue eyes twinkling up at Abel in shared camaraderie, until reaching her climax, the young woman biting her lip to stifle all sound, and when she finished she'd tuck the photograph into her briefs, then press the thumbtack into the door frame, to await its next calling. But the launch of that viewing gallery isn't as 'innocent' as it appears to Abel. It will return to haunt him many years later when he'll witness another young woman jerking off with earplugs blaring, mouthing the words to a song – but that episode almost gets Abel into a world of serious trouble. Masturbation fantasies or not, he'll wish he'd dusted a little more carefully, and never cracked through that ceiling.

Heroism seems to be charged through Abel's playfield's solenoids, his ball shoots off all the bumpers and the numbers in the back glass BING BING to atmospheric heights ... The boss's young son works evenings after school to learn the business, and one very cold night, the boy and a couple of other young employees gather around the central furnace trying to keep warm in this huge, freezing hangar of a warehouse; as the fire dies down, the son starts feeding the furnace empty plastic spools ... He fills it to capacity and when the plastic catches, the furnace begins to radiate red heat, the chimney pipe glows searing white – almost see-through

– on the verge of this pulsating napalm bomb exploding the boss's son panics, and runs to get Abel, the only 'senior' around, whimpering, *If we survive the explosion Dad'll kill me* … Abel yells for all the workers to run out to the car park to the fire assembly point, he grabs a crowbar and, hiding behind a flat carton – as if cardboard would halt the spraying napalm – inches his way towards the searing furnace; as he flicks open the feed door on top, plastic lava spews into the air and burns Abel's arm and hand through the dustcoat and shirt; the furnace lid melts off its hinges and falls, liquid metal spreading across the floor … black smoke fills the warehouse, but with the pressure relieved, soon the fire burns down and the metal casing dims back to black … A drop of the melting lava burned through Abel's sneakers and he hobbles around for a couple of weeks, but it's well worth the discomfort: as a reward for saving the boss's son and the warehouse, come December the big boss lends his large beach-house to three Vietnamese families and Abel to use during the Christmas holidays, free of charge – like *Woo-hoo!* Abel, in his foggy car, slaps away the female voice calling from the back seat, *Abel, Abel,* stinging him like bees, and concentrates on the large house on top of the hill, the tantalising ocean and beach spread below, plus the promenade, the shops, restaurants and of course, South Beach pub where it all happened … The Vietnamese families occupy three bedrooms and Abel has a full bedroom with double bed just for him; the families are nice people, all from work and their kids range from six months to ten years old, nice, polite kids. One of the girls – five years old with big shy eyes, a real little squirrel – reminds him of Rose, so Abel occasionally volunteers to baby-sit this young mob so that the adults can go out for a quiet meal; Abel and the seven kids eat fish and chips and watch television, and for some stupid reason it reminds him of his family's heady Brady-Bunch days before it all went pear-shaped, so now its $M+7\times K$ … On Saturday nights the huge South Beach Hotel, practically perched on the sand, holds a dance, the wide glass doors are flung open, and the entire beach community rocks and rolls for miles around in its blazing party orb, the old wooden building shakes to pieces … Abel snaps his fingers as he sees himself, sweaty, drunk, dancing with one partner after another, 'Jailhouse Rock', 'Long Tall Sally', 'Red River Rock' … then the slow, intimate swaying 'Put Your Head On My Shoulder', 'I'll Never Fall In Love Again' … the girls in short, frilly skirts and teased hair, singing along, swooning in his arms, or standing in groups by the wall, doing little turns, tapping their feet to the music, waiting … Abel blinks, long and slow, as he sees Pam for the first time, rocking and rolling with a girl; Abel, in pointy shoes and stovepipe jeans, is twirling another girl with his arm over her head like a blessing, but the connection to this other strange girl is instant and magnetic, and he snaps stolen glances at every turn. Abel misses his girl's outstretched hand as she spins back to him, and she loses balance, and crashes into another dancing couple, and with a huff storms off, leaving him partnerless in mid-floor … He shrugs and turns both palms over at Pam as she spins and hugs her female partner, short skirt airborne, swivel-ling under the girl's docked hand; she returns him a downcast-eyed grin, and when the bracket is finished they return to their separate corners, Abel to some beer-guzzling blokes, and she to a gaggle of girls, snapping short glances at the guys over their shoulders … Why this girl over all the others? He hasn't a clue then and still doesn't decades later – does the rest of his life make any sense? Not much – Pam isn't the tallest, nor the sexiest nor the prettiest, but it's her, at least for now, at least for this night, she bounces on the spot even without music, hanging onto the other girl's shoulder and laughing … *Go for it*, old Abel hurries youthful Abel along, as though the young man needs prompting – the DJ retakes his place and Abel knows if he hesitates too long he'll miss his chance, so he pushes himself off the wall and joins the throng of boys crossing the floor, *fuck it*, he's too late, another guy has beaten him to her … but wait, she shakes her head, *no thanks* … Abel reaches out and after a long look at her girlfriend she takes his hand – the other girl shrugs and sticks her tongue out – and Abel and Pam rock and twirl, her teased blonde kiss-curls whipping from side to side, the red taffeta skirt crumpling when they crunch together – they chat the basics (name, rank and serial number), by the time the DJ packs up Abel's eyes twinkle with sweaty plans and as Pam's girlfriend comes over Pam says, *I'm going with this bloke, don't wait up*; the girl looks surprised, *You sure?* Pam nods and grips his arm but now there's another problem, no liquor outside the dancehall and the bottle shops are closed, but before the music dies he tells Pamsy – she doesn't seem to mind her new name – *Pamsy, don't worry* – he takes her hand and leads her up the hill, hides her outside the boss's house, he sneaks into the kitchen, and returns with two long cold beer bottles ... Night saved, they descend to the beach where couples and groups dot the sand, the jetty and the rocks, since it's a warm January night, and too much hot blood circulates through Abel's veins as he leads Pam through the night to the end of the beach where the rocks are flat, far enough from the small, festive township, to be in the dark; they sit cross-legged between the wet rocks, passing the beer bottles, giggling into the shadowy sea, the distant sound of the waves comforting like a soft bed. Pamsy is not an experienced drinker, neither is she well versed in what to do next, she seems reluctant, does not respond with moans as some other girls he's been with, but due to his Clara-the-cleaner tuition, Abel is a fair leader, he goes slowly, step by step, and whereas most girls would have complained about the damp sand and hard rocks, Pamsy clutches Abel with both hands and allows him the goal-to-goal freedom, and Abel experiences an epiphany. His body is pumping one way but his mind meanders in another direction; his past life runs against the back of his closed eyes like a fast-forward video – maybe prompted by the Vietnamese kids and their attentive, loving parents – so clearly does he see himself with parents, two sisters and Ginger the kitten on that blissful barbecue afternoon, that he feels that if he opens his eyes he could reach out and touch them. But that scene fades so fast and he's alone, living with Granny Annie, no one even close to his age, no one who knows him enough to lay an intimate, comforting hand on his arm even in silence when the going gets tough. No one to hug and hold and laugh as

Roma has George and George has Roma, and while his body collapses in orgasm, his mind explodes with the sudden understanding that it's more than just for now, more than just for this night, that finally, after losing his family, he's now found a soul mate and regained his place in the world. This is the measure of heroism, not to pull some lost soul up the sheer face of a cliff – kids' stuff – but to find a kindred spirit and have the courage to acknowledge her and pull her towards him … and all because of his banged-up right foot.

Abel sits in the South Beach sauna grinning, what a perfect place to be surrounded by steam. Another man, the publican himself, sits on the opposite bench, sweating, watching the steam stream down in an eerie, fuzzy glow like a boat's fog-lights. *Crikey, is it three years already?* the publican says, and he should know since Abel and Pamsy got married at the South Beach Hotel – only fitting, right? – returning every three years for Christmas holidays when the warehouse is closed, occupying the same honeymoon suite that in many ways charted their lives … Abel knew better than to tell his new wife that married life not only brought him the new family that he'd so missed, much more than that, he felt that he had a soul mate again – just like Dad when young, being understood without too many words – speaking when the mood took, silent for hours when it suited, very much the relationship he'd had with his father, a huge compliment and it really was that relaxed and easy-going with Pamsy from the beginning … They had their *separate* lives and *together* lives: in the mornings they said their farewells, she off to her supermarket job and he to the warehouse; at night they had dinner together, shared a drink and watched TV; sex was not the smorgasbord Abel had imagined of married life – that's not to say that he was ever turned down – there just wasn't the enthusiasm from his wife and he put it down to having been *too* well trained by Clara-the-cleaner to believe that all women wanted it all of the time. Some nights Pam went out with her girlfriends, one of them her dancing partner from the South Beach Hotel that first night, and Abel worked late many nights and of course, Abel had the George-and-Roma parallel universe, sometimes Abel still went on his own to the senior McCullums for tea with the newly married young McCullums, and sometimes to the pinnie basement on his own for quiet contemplation, the steel balls buzzing, and of course later he had his two boys that he spent weekends and all his spare time with having fun. They had just got Wags-Two – a crossbred black and brown beagle, bought a caravan and had started going camping when Abel and Pam returned to the South Beach honeymoon suite for their first three-year anniversary, they had their one-year-old boy with them, the publican could hardly refuse, they did get married there, after all, the three weeks filled with babe on shoulders and squealing-running in and out of the waves, building sand castles and tea at six then watch TV … Six years into married life, another son was added, now they needed the additional bedroom next to the honeymoon suite, but even then, they hardly had any time to themselves, kids up at six-thirty, beach all day, tea at six, falling asleep in front of the TV, they returned home more tired than when they'd arrived, then, on the third time, three years later, not only were they the proud owners of dog and caravan – but they'd suddenly jumped from two to four kids, one baby son just out of the oven and one-fully baked four-year-old girl – just the way the pinball had ricocheted, no use intellectualising it – their new daughter panicked if she woke at night and couldn't see Abel, so Abel slept on a cot in the kids' room … After the kids grew up and left home it was back to the two oldies in the same honeymoon suite … *Twelve times we've been back here, mate, and we're just about due for our thirteenth*, Abel tells the publican through the steam, and *now I'm here visiting on my own because of that damned clock over the pool and that mystery white-clad nurse constantly harassing me … – Do you want to make your next reservation?* the publican wants to know, but they can't talk of it, because the ball hasn't drained and Abel hasn't given a full account of himself. The steam feels so comfortable and familiar but also a bit scary, tingling again with that *what could have been if … if … Jill … Jill …* no use dwelling on that, *I could've, I should've, I would've – but I didn't take the initiative and it didn't happen*, because Abel couldn't wrestle his destiny from the ricocheting pinball's clutches.

Power strike in the state of Victoria, no steam, un-pressed garments piling up with orders in danger of being cancelled if they miss their delivery deadline, serious problem; Abel – above and beyond his role – drives a truck packed with the crushed garments for two and a half hours to Albury in New South Wales where they have plenty of power and steam, then returns two days later to pick them up and drop off another load.

Jack & Jill's Dry Cleaners & Pressing Service is the largest and cheapest in town; business is brisk, customers in and out all day, and even though Jack died some years back, Jill, tall, flat-chested with short, straight black hair, does a sterling job of running the operation. Jill relates to Abel from their first eyeball. Her parents split when young, passed around relatives, not a big talker and hardly ever laughs. Jill chews miniscule gum slowly with a closed mouth, tantalisingly, defused jade eyes sending a direct message with each mastication. After dropping off his garment load, they share a pie and salad in Jill's back office, and talk little but think and listen heaps. After the first week, the pie turns into fresh, home-cooked pasta – different every visit – Jill serves it in her usual sleeveless checked shirt, tiny angel tattoos on both shoulders. And now she even smiles. Hum-de-hum-hum, two lost souls making provisional contact on the playfield until Abel's silver ball hits the blue jet bumper and the solenoid gushes torrential rain that floods all the roads and Abel is unable to drive back home. Seeking Jill's advice on the best, cheapest motel, Jill obliges with an even bigger smile, although her mouth is still clamped: *Save your money, mate, the best and cheapest stay is at my place. Plenty of room and management might even throw in a meal*, her lips stop their rumination and her smile stays out for so long like she's forgotten the retrieval formula. After years of fronting up to the McCullums Abel is well versed in the dinner invitation protocol and when she answers the door he's sporting a bunch of flowers and a box of chocolates ... *You shouldn't have Abel, no need to, honestly – Well, honestly, you saved me the cost of a room and supper.*

Lights are dimmed, candles lit, pots brewing on the stove sending up more steam signals than her pressing tables, and bottle of wine is already uncorked … Her two grown sons come in, shake hands and go out; Jill's smile is doing all the chewing now: *I was a child bride* – could it be that a blush is piggybacking the slow chomping? – *So young that Jack had to sign adoption papers when we got married,* she shrugs foolishly and laughs – WOW, LAUGHS – diffused curtain slipped, jade eyes bare. Two bottles of wine and a delicious meal, Abel feels very sated when he goes to bed in the spare room, lying on his back thinking over the evening, Jill wafts into the dark room, dropping her nightie and laying her long, suntanned body next to his, staring at the same quiet ceiling. More than her nakedness – in the second before Jill shuts the door to the lit-up hallway – her intentions are clearly signalled, *She isn't chewing gum …* After an intense session of quiet, sweaty desperation – Jill pulling all of him in as though to fill a bottomless void – they lie quietly together, Jill's skin radiating a warmth that he only now realises is missing from his wife, and never was there in the first place; Jill puts her hand on his and pressing down gently he can feel her smiling in the dark; neither sleep all night, dozing, watching the wall shadows grow paler … The floods on the highways subside the next day, and clear and sunny days for the rest of the power strike give Abel no excuse to stay over, but he thinks about that sizzling one-night-stand every second of the long drives to and fro, and when they're having their pasta lunch in Jill's office, not much is said but every gentle chewing down of the tight lips and newly-polished jade eyes send more signals than a jungle telegraph, asking Abel to evaluate his relationship with his wife compared to ... he doesn't know exactly what until Abel's last pick-up, after the unions have announced a settlement, Jill lays on the lunchtime table much more than mere lasagne: it's a partnership proposal, equal share of everything, partners in and out of work. *We're a match*, she smiles away, nervously, then languidly smooths out on the table two long, thin matches, with big red heads ... *we're practically identical, Abel, a team.* The business makes plenty of money, why work for someone else, right? Suitable partners, right? In every way, right? Her exact words are: *Made for each other, soul mates, in and out of bed, I have no idea why, but I've never felt stronger about anything all of my life ... if you share my sentiments, come join me and work for yourself ... work for yourself, no more bosses, and hey, won't even need to change the sign out front – JACK & JILL'S – what do you say, JACKSON? ... What do you say, Jacko?* She gets up, one tiny gold earring sparkling, and with wet eyes kisses his cheek then runs her hand through his hair – Pam has never ... Jill sits back down, chomping halted, face pale, grips table edge to steady nerves, pulls drawer open and takes out two sets of keys, one with large attached *Jill* tag, the second with *Jacko*; she slides this second set over to his side, fleetingly brushing his hands ... It's the shortest drive ever back to the warehouse, each kilometre sucked into the jamboree of thoughts racing through Jill's chewing whirlwind proposal. Every intersection he passes has signs like NO MORE BOSSES and JACK & JILL'S DRY CLEANERS & PRESSING SERVICE. Every day Abel thinks of nothing else, every night his mind is in Albury working, eating, fucking, chewing gum, grinning – side by side with Jill, skins burning, her fingers drifting through his hair. One time at work, Abel is mesmerised by a vision: there he is under Granny Annie's house, squashed between the silver caterpillars, thunderstorms crackling over the ocean, listening to a room full of adults discussing his life, his parents, his sisters, his bosses, Abel becomes hot and anxious, he needs to crawl out from that spider-infested limbo world and become an adult, make a grab for the steering wheel, start making his own decisions. What a rare opportunity, to leave his old life behind. What did *Abel* ever do for him? – bugger all, troubles, disappointments, parents separated, bunged-up foot ruined his jewellery job, Mary pregnant blaming Abel, shit job being taken advantage of, a wife that is never, well, physical ... *walk away, mate, leave your old life and its backpack full of troubles behind ...* new life, new identity, new location, new partner, keyset on table beckoning – *You owe* Abel, *nothing, Jackson, NOTHING ... it's high time you tilted the machine and fuck the consequences, sink that silver ball into a bright and glowing future ... this is your last chance, Jackson, grab the jackpot, join Jill, pick up those keys, do it, Jacko, just do it!*

In the South Beach Hotel's bar, between the shelves of bottles and glasses, hangs a corkboard with thirteen pictures, each one documenting the Marvin family's visits to the hotel, the first is their wedding, the others of the return anniversaries, of course missing on the board is their first dance and first coupling, but that glorious night is forever stamped on Abel's mind ... Memory is a bit fuzzy but old Abel believes he's here to revisit what happened on their second anniversary visit, when they weren't confident of leaving their older boy and new baby with a babysitter, so one night Pam went out on her own, a second night, just before the end of the holidays, it was his turn but he convinced Pam to go out again, then he brings in the arranged babysitter, the publican's teen daughter, and sneaks downstairs to surprise her, but Pamsy isn't in the bar. When Abel asks about her, he meets only averted eyes, he nods at her profile on the corkboard, *That's the woman I'm talking about* ... now even more shrugs and downcast glances, but on his way out of the bar the publican, visibly nervous, whispers, *Check out the beach under the small, northern jetty* ... Abel thinks he must've misheard – *that's Poofy's Hideaway, right?* – but the advice is right on the money, he makes his way along the dark sands to the jetty at the far end of the beach and almost stumbles on a couple between two columns, the lighthouse's rotating beam highlights the back of Pamsy's black quilted vest and her raised naked bottom half, head buried between another moaning woman's naked thighs ... like a video tape being slowly rewound, Abel retreats backwards, eyes glued to his wife's half-naked body, with downcast eyes he hustles through the lobby and back upstairs to the honeymoon suite; when Pam returns she speaks, something about a stroll with a new girlfriend, but her averted eyes and the shakiness of her voice tell Abel that the second woman must've recounted his sudden silent appearance in the passing lighthouse beam, and Pam has worked out it must have been Abel ... The rest of the holiday is a prison of silence, Abel unable to clear his head and think logically about anything else.

When they get back home Abel packs his things and moves them into his room at Product Line Warehouse, the bosses allow their star employee to use their personal showers and so Abel's workplace becomes his home as well. Again, he has lost his family, and he only sees his two boys occasionally, they scream and clutch when he leaves them, but this is one set of CLANG CLANG DING DING DING WOOOP WOOOP WAAK WAAK OWOWOWOWOW that even the most fierce machine-tilting can do nothing about. In the deserted warehouse at night, sitting in silence on his army cot – bashing his head against the wall till he bleeds and passes out is what he should be doing – *I had a chance to change my life, had a chance to dump Abel and become Jackson and instead I bucked my destiny like the Buckaroo bronco, and kicked myself in the head.* He should've joined Jill, he'd hit *jackpot* and was too chickenshit to collect, should have let that slow, rhythmic chewing suck him into its swirl of promise, *Jacko … Jacko …* And why didn't he pick up those keys? An abhorrent reluctance to break up his family? A shuddering nightmare of Jacko dragging Abel's two sons into the car every second weekend when leaving Albury, the boys crying for the long drive back, the vision of his two squirrels clutching his legs – a father, under whatever name – when he dropped them back to their mother's place, Wags-Two bounding to comfort his two crying masters, caravan sitting disused, parked in street. And what has he got now, fuck all, same old Abel, working for others for the rest of his life, his family broken, his boys traumatised. What in his being keeps hurtling him back to this profound loneliness? Snippets of an old song, about reality and loneliness cutting a man to pieces, taunt him … His scalp prickles, craving Jill's touch, not even once did he get to see that elusive, miniature gum, jade eyes mirrored in the glinting earring so frontal in his memory that he cries, pounding his fist into the soft bed.

That special sweetie aroma rising from the blue tray as the Glad Wrap is lifted off, the perfume of Granny Annie's memory, still invades Abel's nostrils, but every day that he lives in the warehouse it fades, and he feels Granny Annie's ghost – with a disapproving frown – slipping away. She left him her large house, in which he was living with Pamsy and his two boys – and his heart aches to be in front of the warm, glowing huge fireplace, with his two boys cuddling and watching TV. Instead he's stuck in the cold warehouse in front of an electric heater with two glowing red bars. His mother is still alive, and so are his sisters, but he can't approach them with this problem, and his father is so far off the radar that contact hasn't even crossed Abel's mind. But he has his *new* extended de facto family, so after two weeks of solitary warehouse living Abel sits in the pub, watching the cold and drizzle outside, just a few degrees above zero and winter hasn't even officially started yet, George rugged up to the eyeballs with coat and scarf comes in, his face and body are heavier – Abel won't discover why until some years later – George unwraps his bulk and wheezes into an inhaler, and they have a beer and after the usual inquiries Abel, looking down, tells George that he's walked out on his wife and family because of her detour to the jetty on their holiday – *Poofy's Hideaway* – Abel can hardly get the words out, so George studies his beer glass as he thinks this over, and even old Abel averts his eyes, thinking confessing to Granny Annie would've been easier – what would Granny Annie have said had she still been alive? Maybe: *Sometimes, some things in life can't be exactly how you want them to be.* He tells George that in retrospect he was plain stupid not to have seen it, that Pam was, well, *underwhelmed* in what he'd expected between husband and wife, and sure, Pam went out with girls occasionally and there were a couple of girls that visited at home when Abel worked late and were still there sharing a drink when he came home, so what? And they hugged a little too closely when departing, so what? Women are more touchy-feely in public, aren't they? *I don't know, I just don't know ...* As it turns out George is in the Granny Annie ballpark, he talks of compromises – all marriages have them – he and Roma have them, and they are, in fact, the basis for a long-lasting relationship – *People just are different in some ways ... you know, Abel? ... and being married, doesn't make them all the same.* No way, this is where George and Granny Annie's therapy parts company, Granny Annie wouldn't have intellectualised this break-up. She'd have said *TWADDLE* then given Abel a smack across the back of his head, she would've expected more of her grandson than to repeat his parents' errant ways and break up his family over nonsense – *nonsense!* Meanwhile, George is continuing his dissertation: *If most of the marriage is sound, if they have lots to share, if they can smile and mean it when they say good morning, if they're there for each other, if they take delight in their children ...* (George stumbles over that last one) *what is a little personal difference? ...*

more interesting, really – blah, blah, blah – *Is George muttering to me or himself?* Abel asks his reflection ... and it's only after George is kicked by the horse, only after that session with Roma in the pinnie basement, that Abel realises that maybe George *was* talking to himself, reconciling not being able to have children, gaining all that weight during treatments – clutching at his manly honour, Abel reminds George again that Pam blatantly goes out for girls' nights and has girls over, et cetera – *You come to Mum and Dad's for dinner and play pinnies till late, don't you?* counters George. *Space, Abel, personal space ... the essential ingredient in a marriage ...* Abel's blood is rising – this *isn't* the same space, she *fucks* other women – but what unnerves Abel, then and now, young and old, is that it feels like Granny Annie is sitting next to George in the bar having a beer, speaking out of George's mouth: *Twaddle, twaddle, twaddle – stop being silly, Abel, you're a family man with responsibilities ...* Even now, old Abel grins into young Abel's depression – can George see Granny Annie's bulk balancing on the stool next to him? He should, George loved Granny Annie's sweetie tray and quoted her mantra in an article on her, the headline on page five, over Granny Annie's photo: *A tray of sweeties to balance out the nasties of life ...* Being a newspaper celebrity made Granny Annie's charity work so much easier, but she warned George with a wave of her wooden baking spoon that eating too many sweeties would kill him one day; George, sidling up to Granny Annie in her kitchen, pinched her cheek and said, *I'm going to make you a star, Granny Annie. You're the protagonist of my next sci-fi series in Dad's paper, called:* 'Mass Murder by Sweeties'. Granny

Annie pinched George's cheek, leaving flour imprints, Abel watched, secretly thrilled that George liked his only viable family member. *It's okay to eat my cakes, George, but in moderation … eat right eighty per cent of the time, then play up for twenty per cent. Eat right and exercise.* George laughed, *I tried bike riding, Granny Annie, look where it got me … dangling off a cliff like jellyfish bait …* Abel told George that when he was little he thought of his granny as one big pulsating heart … *Yeah, right!* George'd laugh: *A heart of pastry …* Now in the bar adult George is saying into his beer: *The imperfection of marriage … sometimes makes both partners try harder … Pam's a good woman, right?* George is just repeating old Abel's own thoughts that young Abel is refusing to acknowledge. How true that was, how absolutely accurate, but young Abel sitting next to George doesn't realise it yet, but old Abel, snuggling back in the steamy car, knows that George called it perfectly, Pam turned out to be much more than a mere *good woman*, she became a bloody saint – but at the time, Abel just swallowed hard and stayed put living in the warehouse, scanning the daily papers for a flat to rent. And old Abel knows the sweeties did not kill George; no one, not even the ghost of Granny Annie with all her life's pointers, could foretell the train of events that would again rob Abel of his dwindling new family.

A month later Abel rides in the car to Melbourne with George and Roma to see an American jazz sextet that George sells as *the hottest sound on the scene. These cool cats'll blow you away, Abel,* which isn't all that bad a proposition since Abel wouldn't mind having his head blown away or at least blasted out clean, crammed as it is with images of his wife's naked backside and her strange new loyalty, and worse, much worse, Abel torn by his two squirrel sons crying, *Daddy, Daddy, don't go* – clinging just like his sisters had hung onto his father – and the silence between him and his wife when he picks up and drops off the boys is crammed, just *how much* can be said without uttering one word is astounding. Has his new family let him down like his old one? Is he *family-less* again? At work he's silent and moody, he's stopped relating to the warehouse staff – where can he go and what can he do? – even less is said during the long silent hours at night in the warehouse. No amount of jumpers can keep him warm, inside and out. Back downstairs to his cubicle, Abel lies on the narrow cot watching the flickering small TV. He can't help but think of the contrast: winter evenings in front of the fire watching TV at home, boys cuddle into him on both sides, his arms around them hugging them closer, Pamsy surveying her kingdom with a smile outshining the glowing fireplace and it totally reminds Abel of George's words – she is trying, *she is …* They watch *Gilligan's Island*, *The Flintstones*, laughing, munching chips and popcorn, the boys fall asleep, he picks them up and carries them to bed, tucks them in, and they sigh, long sighs of security and contentment. Finishing beer with Pamsy, soft clink go the glasses, *You're a good daddy, Abel Jackson Marvin – I've finally created the world around me I was robbed of …* The four of them plus dog camping by a creek – nothing if not full of dizzying flashbacks to his youth – they run, fish and chase Wags-Two. Pam, a country girl, a wizard with a campfire, her camp-pot-roast legendary, bending over the fire gently prodding the suckling meat, its smell like an escaped genie saturating the trees, the boys dancing around with hunger – *Not long now, boys,* she winks at Abel, *good things are worth waiting for.* Kids tucked into their sleeping bags, Pamsy and Abel sit side by side, having a drink, watching the fire burn down. Four of them in sleeping bags inside the tent, dog cuddling up for warmth ... In the car Roma turns to give him a long searching look, melancholy not befitting him – he hasn't seen Roma since he moved out, has George told her about him and Pam? – Abel wishes he had, maybe she could touch him with those life-giving hands and all would be well again – old Abel feels only a shudder of guilt, the nurse's voice behind him thick and strong: *Does this full account include your best friend, or best enemy?* – Once they get to the concert hall George and Roma bounce in their seats, clapping and whooping; Abel tries to follow, but the sounds are loud and abstract, each instrument blasts on its own, the sextet rarely playing the same tune that he can recognise. He misses that mellow, regimented Swing jazz George had taught him. This concert is a noise fest, Abel's head is crammed with his crying two boys, he just wants to go home. He struggles on until the saxophonist hushes the crowd between numbers – *Had an interview with Miles Davis for a gig some time back ... yeah ... You know Mr Davis here in Melbourne, right? Is he as big here as in the US?* (Loud cheers and applause, even a rookie like Abel knows Miles Davis, George idolises him) ... *Right on. Mr Bebop, Mr Cool Jazz – one of the most influential musicians of this century ... yeah ... well, after the interview*

Mr Miles asked me onto the bandstand where the other cool cats were waiting to see what I've got … yeah … we were going to have a jam session right there … yeah … and Mr Miles asked me, 'You ready, Daddio?' … I looked around and there was no score, no list, no instructions, the cats just fiddling with their instruments anxious to take off. – Abel slouches, thinks, *No instructions? Sounds like my life. I sprung my mother then my wife. No instruction on how to handle either* – The jazz man continues: *Yeah … and I said, 'Man, what do you want me to play?' and he said … Mr Miles said, 'Man, play what you hear, Daddio' … Cool, right? So the cats and Miles blasted off with … you know what? … This'll blow you away, those cats exploded into the theme from* The Odd Couple *… Can you believe that? … You have that TV show here, in Australia, right? You know that comedy show? You know that theme* … (he blows a few notes – tat tat tat … ta ta) … *And like, man, they did not blow out a mild and funny comedy show, no siree, they blew some serious fully blown shit – excuse me – I was a little shaken, man … more surprised and scandalised, I'd say … yeah … like, I had no space in* my *jazz world for that twiddle dee twiddle dum theme music from a funny TV show, right? It was like, no way, man,* The Odd Couple? *… Give me a break … But then, man, I forgot what I knew, forgot what I'd felt – like man, forgot my prejudice* … (he laughs long, deep big white teeth and wet red gums) … *and I did what my music guru Mr Miles advised me to do … I listened … I shook the wax out of my ears, lifted myself up … I LISTENED … and you know what, I heard it, it went into me, I felt it and I started playing what I heard and when that gig was finished, I was a better musician … yeah … a better man than I'd* *been before … Yeah,* The Odd Couple … *here it is for you, Melbourne …* The Odd Couple … Abel shakes himself awake to the theme of his and Pamsy's favourite TV show, and those six guys deconstruct the music then put it back again, blowing individual tantrums, racing off on their own tangents, but when the final notes are gently placed and tucked down, nothing has really changed, it's the same old tune … They buy the band's tape and play it on their way home, Roma is driving while George taps out the tunes on the dashboard and when the tape plays *The Odd Couple* theme Abel asks, *What did Mr Miles mean by: play what you hear?* and George says, *He means use your intuition. Instinct, perception, awareness; interpret the music to your own vocabulary.* And there Pam is at home on a Sunday arvo – old and young Abel see her so clearly – cooking and freezing for the week while Abel and his two sons build a massive Lego structure in the middle of the floor, younger son knocks down a tower, older son yells in indignation – *Abel, Abel, Abel* – for better or worse, there is no *Jackson* and there never was – Abel shakes the wax out of his ears, lifts himself up and he hears it. The next day after work he packs his things and moves back home.

High season, Abel – promoted to assistant manager after the Albury pressing initiatives – works half days on Saturdays, then goes to the pub, downs a couple of beers, and scans the paper – how uninteresting, downright boring *The Prospector* has become since George was injured, no quirky articles to win the hearts and minds of his readers – still no word from George or Roma, Abel's heart aches every time he thinks about them, every time he picks up *The Prospector*. The paper brings back the warm glow of his family 'golden' age, the recent one – that long-ago family joy when he was a boy has retreated so far back Abel would indeed need to be a prospector to connect with it again. The 5×M+D photo, even though it still occupies prime position in the lounge room, is no longer his primary nostalgic angle of repose. But what he thinks about as he sips his beer is the modern golden family, when he Pamsy and the two boys were living with Granny Annie, and his extended family was just within reach, Roma, George and George's parents and Chief Frank. Now Granny Annie is dead, he broke up then moved back with Pamsy but things have not yet gone back as they were – and may never do so, the disassociation stays with him – George and Roma have disappeared out of his life for three years and all he has left is *The Prospector* minus George's sardonic articles … At work he stares at the framed Bravery Award, so much promise then, on the verge of a new world of friendship, and now they've gone, vanished. There is Abel again climbing down the rocks on that sheer cliff drop. He hangs onto the stretched-out jeans, pushing from his mind any consequences should they unravel, break, come apart … then the grand prize, much more than the Bravery Award, first sight of Roma in the amusement arcade, striding in, confident of who she is and where she's going, hands on hips, pulling Abel closer and kissing him on the lips, *Thank you for saving my George* – only to end up hiding somewhere with her crippled husband – every time he thinks of this, damned often – it's always dog-tailed by that damned ghost of a white nurse that has been stalking him since Roma fired off the silver ball and this escapade in the steamy car started. Is this the white-clad nurse's payback for his question: *If you save a life, are you responsible for it?* He actually asked her, didn't he? He wasn't just asking himself, right? It drives old Abel crazy in the steamy car, but he still can't identify this white apparition sitting in silence allowing that quandary to surface and sink in; he asks himself again louder, blocking out the nurse: *DID I DO ENOUGH TO SAVE GEORGE? WAS IT MY FAULT HE GOT CRIPPLED?* Being wedged in that storm of silence in George's room after quoting Alfred E Neuman's motto, *What, me worry?* he should've seen it coming, should've gone along to the demo with his friend, should've anticipated, should've *felt* George's anxiety, his next move, that his friend would never be satisfied unless he was in the frontline of protest no matter how violent it turned out. George was a book nerd, an intellectual, he wasn't street smart, no matter how many times he'd stood shoulder to shoulder with Roma as she teased the Buckaroo horse to buck and kick – George didn't understand that if you get too close to a spooked horse they'll buck and twist and kick you in the head. George knew nothing and saw nothing except his righteousness; democracy was on his side, so how could he go wrong? He was the good guy, nothing would happen to him, with thousands like him they'd bring down the bad guys … *But I knew better, didn't I? I knew that the bad guys can win and just walk away. My mum and dad did it, I did it after I tumbled Bernie down the stairs …* He should've been at George's side, protecting him, he should have wrapped his arms around him and pulled his friend out of harm's way. He sees himself doing it, over and over, clamping hands on George's ample shoulders and yanking him back, both laughing ... *Remember Buckaroo?* That's what best friends are for, right? Saving George's life once wasn't enough: his rescuer went missing the second time he was needed. Abel sips his beer ... *Chicken any good?* ... Tanned thigh eases onto the stool next to him, wrapped in gaping avocado-green cloth, feet in worn sandals: *Is the chicken here any good?* ... light from the open doorway shines a halo behind her head, *Hi, I'm Papaya*, she extends her hand, and after a moment's hesitation, *Hi, Abel* ... he scans the empty stools along the bar, this angel is talking to me for a reason. *I'm from Christmas Hills, the other side of Melbourne, the Children of Peace –* Oh God, she's a Mormon freak, he half-turns away, but her crinkled blue-eyed smile draws him back – *We have a farm there called The Shelter ... have you heard of us?* What are the odds? His pinball must have bounced off the right bumper this morning, George McCullum's old 'Children of Peace' article springs to mind, them and their avocado-coloured sheets and names comprised of fruit and veggies – *should be called The Fruitcakes*, George had laughed – Papaya interrupts with an angel's whisper, *We look after damaged people ... and lonely, depressed people; we offer them peace and quiet to give their bodies and minds a chance to cure themselves* – Abel nods, this attractive woman seems to have all the time in the world to talk to strangers – *I'm here to deliver a message to Sir Marvin-the-Magician from Dame Gypsy-of-the-Romani – any idea where I can find this chivalrous knight?* She paints the mirror with one of her special angelic beams ... *She'd really like to see you,*

Abel. She needs you … It has been three years since Roma and George disappeared – George's parents and Roma's father have deflected Abel's desperate concern at every phone call (when Roma was ready she'd contact Abel). Even *The Prospector* had gone cold on the subject … Abel swallows, asks, *How's George? – Peaceful …* – they face off in the mirror – *No improvement, I'm sorry.* Abel looks into his drink, Roma's black eyes stare back at him, *He doesn't recognise me … can't speak … can't walk …* Papaya waits until Abel looks back at her in the mirror: *Roma is ready for you to meet your daughter … Acacia …*

On this muggy Saturday morning Abel readies himself to visit George … old Abel repeats the words with young Abel: *Is he any better?* Pam looks on, things still cool between them, *You're a good man, Abel Jackson Marvin. You saved his life on that cliff – But for what? … For what?* he asks – *Without you he would not have married Roma, they would not have had all those happy years together.* Abel is still not convinced, so his wife tries harder … *They're a couple, George is lucky to have such a devoted partner looking after him.* Pamsy doesn't mention children, she knows they've been trying unsuccessfully since they got married. Pamsy doesn't know about that night in the pinnie basement – if she did, she'd have put it down to payback for her *Poofy's Hideaway* excursion. But of course she'd have been dead wrong. When the cape-draped Roma pulled Abel down on top of her, his wife's indiscretion was the last thing on his mind. Abel had thought that the night of making love to Roma would retreat, with no other traces than a warm and fuzzy glow – although anyone knowing the stunning Roma would find that laughable … But things are different now, the one-night-stand spawned a love child – *Come and meet your daughter, Abel* … Abel chews this over on the long drive, and by the time he gets to Eltham heavy black clouds threaten, forecasting imminent disaster. Weaving his way up the narrow Kangaroo Ground Road, sheets of water tumble, thudding down on the station wagon, thunder cracks like a cattle-rustler's whip and lightning slashes the black sky – Pamsy's response perhaps when she finds out about his illegitimate child? Abel grinds his way up the hill, and at the top the car emerges from the dense cloud, as though the storm had spat it out – like a soul flung to heaven – *Maybe Papaya is an angel, and this is heaven?* Abel muses – the now-clear sky is layered in shades of blue, in the far distance are the Dandenongs, still battered by lightning … *Papaya and the Children of Peace,* George laughed after Abel read his article, *more like Children of Thieves … They take in these sick, depressed people and milk them for all their money; their leader, that sweet angelic Papaya, has already been sued for changing wills,* George laughed again, *Rather than The Shelter they should call it The Milking Shed.* – Abel points down at the article: *It doesn't say anything like that.* – *It did,* replied George, *Dad took it out* … George mimics his father: *No editorialising, son, those are just allegations, let the story speak for itself.* – Roma didn't share George's views: *They're decent, gentle people performing a community service, no one else takes in these … rejects.* And now both – all three of them – are *rejects,* George, Roma and … and Roma's daughter, Acacia … As instructed by Papaya, he swings sharply onto a narrow dirt track … *Poor George,* he thinks, *it's going to be difficult seeing him, but Roma …* – his heartbeat ramps up a notch, he hasn't seen her since that night, since she pulled him down with all her clawing strength, capes spread on the floor – *Those hands, those magical hands … maybe she'll touch my face …* At the first sight of The Shelter Abel gets out of the car and understands why broken people would live here. The farm is a perfect mirage of heaven, hills and hills of luscious green; fields, trees and buildings glisten from the recent downpour, the sun shines Biblical shafts from the blue tiled sky upon blossoming trees, large sunflowers twist their heads to the light, people labour in the vegetable fields – he imagines he hears them singing – cows graze, and children frolic – what had George called it after his journalistic visit? *Shangri-La, mate, the lost paradise.* Abel slowly drives the narrow, slippery path down the hill and slows to read: *Children of Peace and Friends of the Earth. All welcome*, then negotiates down the rest of the steep hill, parks and gets out, the sun in the valley stinging his face like tiny arrows, so Abel wishes he had his Roma sunglasses. He squints at the strange procession of people coming towards him all wearing avocado-coloured sheets, and he remembers George's *Macbeth* quote in his article: *As I did stand my watch upon the hill, I looked down toward Birnam, and anon methought, the wood began to move …* and Abel had worn a shirt and tie to make a good first impression. The avocado people, loudly singing and clapping, surround Abel; a familiar face – Papaya – approaches, *Thank you so much for coming, Abel*, kissing him on both cheeks before rescuing the daunted man from the forest horde, and leading him towards a long, low, log building – *The dining room, we'll have lunch here as soon as you've connected with your family – My family?* Abel swallows; Papaya points further up the path, pats his shoulder and walks away ... Old Abel in the steamy car goes weak as he takes in this whirling, ethereal, fantasy that is Roma, her loose white dress and bare feet, plaited black hair hanging down her back like a rope, she radiates sunshine, merging into the surrounding jungle of camellias, lavender and magnolia, more powerful than anything he's imagined on the two-and-a-half-hour drive from home ... Roma pushes George down a tricky gravel path in a bulky white wheelchair; she stops, shields her eyes, then as she spots Abel, she jumps up, waves and waves, coiled hair bouncing ... then Abel starts running, feet barely touching the ground ... this wraithlike vision of flowers and sunshine clamps arms around Abel and cries years of demon tears, and when she stops weeping, she kisses Abel on his lips, just as she did the first time they met, then strokes his face, *Thank you for coming ...* A little naked girl has stopped playing in the sandpit and has straightened up; head tilted she watches, as though she has never seen her mother do that before, then she shoots out of the blocks and covers the distance in seconds flat, the little naked wet savage, smudged with sand, hat flying off as she takes a running leap right on top of them, grabbing the two hugging adults, and the three cling together in the sunshine ... *Acacia, meet your daddy ... Daddy Abel, meet your daughter ...* Inside this whirlwind, tears flood Abel's eyes as they disentangle, and he looks to George, but his wheelchair-bound friend only slumps over sideways, nodding to himself ... *Sir*

George-of-the-Jungle, mate, it's Sir Marvin-the-Magician, how're you doing? ... Abel straightens his friend up, takes his hand and looks into his eyes, but finds only vacancy, no laughter, no sarcasm – *No one home, George has gone missing ... missing in Shangri-La, the lost paradise.*

Abel sits in the steamy car in front of Welfare House, not a lot has changed over the past forty years, the hangar-like structure may have been repainted, and the doors and windows had a facelift, but the rest is the same, still on the edge of town in a disused warehouse, its huge hall set up with trestle tables and benches, a large, industrial kitchen and a row of toilets; as soon as the front doors are opened the shabby *mates and dearies* still enter en masse with bent backs, hungry eyes and shaking hands, and leave a couple of hours later, picking their teeth with relaxed faces and patting their full bellies ... When Granny Annie can no longer drive, Abel drives her extensive bulk and her sweeties to Welfare House; getting her out of the Mini, Granny Annie jokes, might require a crane ... Once out of the Mini, Granny Annie straightens up, dusts off, and marches in like a general to inspect her troops; Abel trails behind, wheeling the luggage trolley with a pyramid of cardboard boxes. As Abel stands to one side, he watches his grandmother take charge. She sets up her sweetie table, covers the cakes with white cheesecloth, smacking away adventurous hands; Abel, leaning back in the car, eyes filling with warm tears, watches the unfortunates shuffle in as the front doors swing open, every day the same bent-over bodies and unshaven faces, the same hesitating shuffle as they push their way to the tables ... faces matter very little, or as Granny Annie puts it: *They have one communal hungry face* ... Nothing changes when Abel takes over after Granny Annie's gone, except that he now drives the station wagon, and the goods are bought not baked – who has the time to bake with four kids running around? – but the rest, even now, is the same, the one common face, the same musky smell – it still fills his steamy nostrils inside the car all those years later – then the hungry eyes lift to watch him in the kitchen and their cracked lips part in a smile, *Thanks, mate ... thanks, dearie ...* Apron-draped Abel returns their smiles, then turns to face his armoury, the routine revolves like a merry-go-round: slice, toast, spread, crack, beat, melt, soak, fry, turn, fry, dish ... and start over again, for two to three hours, depending on the turnout, the hunger levels, the cold outside ... *Thanks, mate ... thanks, dearie ...* as they shuffle past on their way out he turns briefly with a smile – *No worries, you have a good one* – and from the corner of his eye sees them face the outside reality, straightening up as they prepare to take on one more day ... One day, one of the old guys – he looks ancient but it's impossible to tell – topples over backwards just as a plate of dripping French toast is placed before him; Abel and another volunteer rush to him, the man's right hand clutches his heart but his left reaches out from the floor towards the table – the covered plates of sweeties shimmering at him – *That's mine, that's my dessert*, the man mumbles, eyes fixated on the plate; he grabs Abel's arm and tries to pull himself upright, Abel clutches the man's worn lapels and lifts him back into his chair, the old man reaches over the French toast and ploughs his savage fingers through the Glad Wrap and shoves a lamington into his toothless mouth, another sweetie in each hand, smacking lips with delight, *Thanks, mate,* the man says. Wiping the white coconut crumbs from his mouth, he smacks Abel on the back, then plants something into Abel's hand: *Wancha to have this, mate.* – Abel looks down astounded, it's a ceramic white angel with one blue wing sticking straight up – *It'll bring you luck …* Abel tries to return it, but the man keeps pushing it back, *No worries, mate, you have a good one, you hear?* Abel intends to return it the next day, frantically searching the old codgers' faces, but the man never returns … *For crying out loud,* Abel whacks the steam angrily, *what else could I have done to give a full account of myself? Lay off me, will you?* – he rebuffs the white-clad nurse – *give me a break, I helped in that place for years. What do I need to do to exorcise that charred contraption from my chest? … I even put that one-winged white angel to good use, didn't I?*

Pull the pin, hear the ping, silver ball bounce and ding … Roma sings, bent over pinball machine, pulls back the plunger and sends Abel spinning, spinning, spinning all over the playfield until he hits the drop target of his retirement party at the warehouse. It's Friday afternoon: Abel, assistant manager, is well versed in all functions of the warehouse, and a friend with these current owners since they were little kids brought to work by mummy and daddy … These new, grown-up young bosses applaud Abel's longevity in this position, not only forty years, but the first *and* last job, the *only* job of a lifetime. On display are both of Granny Annie's framed hero articles under glass, George's rescue and the Bravery Award presentation; next to them a blowup of Captain Marvel struck by lightning with Abel's face superimposed on it – *This is your life, Marvin Shazam*. Pamsy, sitting next to her husband, clinks glasses, beaming with pride … With the staff all gathered, eating drinking and celebrating, the managers recount some of the mad 'adventures': Abel's sharp about-turn during the hold-up, the story of how Abel helped a young mum give birth to a boy when her waters suddenly broke (resulting in the only Vietnamese boy with the middle name of *Abel*), Abel's heroism during the plastic spool fire – the young boss clinks glasses with Abel, *You saved my arse, mate* … And so on and so on, so many yarns to fill his forty-year work tapestry, everyone laughing including Abel, who won't spoil this merrymaking by divulging his observations from the ladies' toilet ceiling. But the white-clad voice in the back of old Abel's car is not placated by the *hooray for Abel* stories: *Have you given a full account of yourself?* Old Abel stops to ponder that request anew … *What else do you want? This is my retirement party, lay off!* … He returns to his party with a tiresome shrug. One side-effect of stealthily spying from that ceiling was that he becomes the sole witness to a secret monthly meeting … yes indeed … on the first Monday of every month – after knock-off time – Abel notices two men slinking into the ladies' toilet block; one day he calmly parks his wheeled caboose and, smooth as a stalking cat, silently climbs up the back of the toilets, weaving through the stacks of cartons, lying down in the thick dust, eye to the peephole, just in time to see the boss give the union rep Abel's signed monthly safety document plus a thick envelope filled with cash; the union guy laughs, *Ha! Hiring the Bravery Award-winning Aussie as the safety officer, pure brilliance!* – he arranges the hundred-dollar notes in neat little piles – *If someone gets crushed by a forklift, or is cooked by boiling steam, far better if an old-fashioned brave Aussie is in charge …* But Abel does nothing, just keeps handing in his signed safety reports, to the detriment of one female employee who isn't present at Abel's retirement party. The voice in the back of the car – *Abel … Abel …* – is lulled, it wants to hear out this full story … Years later the effects of those meetings come into play during a lengthy wharf strike: ships ride anchor in Port Melbourne like the D-Day armada, and when the strike ends the ships disgorge containers at breakneck speed, semi-trailer after semi-trailer arrives at the warehouse, unloading mountains of goods, the staff work early starts and night shifts to clear the backlog, and Abel struggles with where to stack these hundreds of pallets, directing whizzing forklifts to disgorge their loads in every corner, and when he runs out of corners, he gets instructions from the boss to stack the pallets in the aisles atop of *KEEP THIS SPACE CLEAR AT ALL TIMES* signs, narrowing passages, high piles of stacked cartons leaning over precariously … a young mother doing her toilet business with Walkman plugs stuffed in her ears, an Asian singer's picture in white suit tacked on the wall, she shuts her eyes, and wistfully sways, mouthing the lyrics, and when she's finished she swoons her dreamy way out of the ladies', plugs implanted in ears, eyes half closed still dreamingly mouthing the words, doesn't hear the clanging sound, vision still full of the singer's image, she doesn't see the spinning yellow light, and is knocked down by a whizzing forklift ... By the time the ambulance turns up, Abel has instructed the blocked aisles around the accident be cleared, and by the time the Work Care investigators and union rep arrive the next morning, all the other aisles have been emptied ... The young mother dies on her way to the hospital. Emergency conference in the boss's office, only the family and Abel present, faces furrowed with worry – *Those aisles were kept clear, right, Abel? ... To the maximum required safety level?* – Abel thumbs his nose, *Well, you told me* – *Never mind that, the family will be well looked after ... you know that, don't you?* – boss breathes slow and steady, sipping a whiskey – *If we're closed down because of negligence, one-hundred and eighty people are out of work. Most don't even speak English, all have families ...* Abel sips his whiskey, tastes it for the next few days, thinking it over. Granny Annie and George are no longer around; Abel goes to see Chief Frank, the retired policeman, Roma's dad. They sit upstairs drinking beer, but Abel feels the tug of the pinnies downstairs ... *This is the story, Frank. I need to go before the Work Care negligence investigating committee and sign a Stat Dec to state that the aisles were kept clear at all times* – *You were full up?* – *Chock-a-block, Frank, packed to the rafters.* The retired police chief thinks it over. *They are good people, Frank, they look after their staff. Bend over to help them, personally, financially, with family and kids, free child-minding centre on site* – *They told you to use the keep clear spaces? You'd be putting your head on the chopping block?* Nodding from Abel, *Haven't slept all that well since it happened. Circumstances, accident ... she walked into that forklift, Frank, blind and deaf – Snitch? – Don't think so, Frank, it's a closed shop* … The daughter of that knocked-down mother, playing in the child-minding centre that night, now a lawyer, sits quietly during the speeches at Abel's farewell, bored expression – *Has she ever wondered who paid her university fees? – But this doesn't make up for losing a mother,* that damned nuisance, white-clad nurse points out, *the woman whose life was snuffed out by that forklift had no time to give a full account of herself, no time to hug her child goodbye* … Is this what this vagabond ghost is after? A life for a life? The pains in his chest – that had been improving steadily – tighten up again with this recollection and his whole body cramps up … *Roma, please, let that bloody ball drain and it'll be all over.*

When they have their first grandchild, Pamsy and Abel have to decide what names they'll be called; Pamsy picks 'Granny Pamsy', and since this new first grandchild is named Annie – in honour of we all know who – Granny Pamsy seems a suitable title. For new Granddad Abel it isn't that easy: 'Granddad', 'Gramps', 'Pop' just don't do it for him so he picks *Jacko* – Pamsy thinks it's a little odd and over-the-top – but she has been warned by friends that it is just a strange new grandpa phase, *best to just humour him.* After all, what does it matter? … Actually it matters to Abel quite a lot – it keeps alive the flickering thrill of almost having dumped *Abel* and resurfacing as the masked *Jacko*, daunted by nothing, not even the breaking up of a family. And every time one of the new grandkids is finally able to put a name to the tall, smiling lamington-offering, swing-pushing apparition, spluttering *Ja-ac-o … Joko … Aaako … Jacko!* their delight is only a smidgen of their grandfather's as he cackles himself silly ... But old Abel isn't laughing now as he tries to relax – absorbing the acute pains in the steamy car – thoughts of Jacko pitch him into the first two weeks of retirement after leaving Product Line. The voices of today belong to three of his beloved grandkids, and as they call out *Jacko, Jacko,* they forewarn: trouble ahead. The first two scheduled Monday morning swims are easy enough, no more hurrying to get to work, then dinner at the pub with neighbours, Tuesday lectures for the retired. Wednesdays are hectic, baby-sitting grandkids, splitting the load of seven with Pamsy, also now retired, Abel takes them to beaches and parks and now he's the sweetie pusher, dosing them up to their eyeballs with sugar, Thursdays bowling and lunch, and Fridays split the shopping with Pamsy. Then the nostalgic highlight, Saturday and Sunday mornings at Welfare House feeding the *mates* and *dearies,* the ghost of Granny Annie hovering like an inspecting general ... but then *Jacko ... Jacko ...* at the end of the second week when they take some grandkids to Orange to visit Pam's family, innocent enough an excursion, right? *NO, no, no,* old Abel waves a warning finger through the steam as he does to his youngest grandkids, they stop in Albury for lunch and walking through the mall the oldest grandchild yells out loudly as only a six-year-old can, *JACKO!* pointing at a large photograph in the window of a dry cleaner's shop. Grandson is, of course, right, even though it was *Jacko* of long ago, eyes crinkling on the verge of a smile, and the name above the establishment says in bold black letters *Jack & Jill's Dry Cleaners etc, etc* ... Abel – as the cliché goes – could have been knocked over with a feather, not only because it is in a totally different location to the original business, nor the highly unlikely nature of the same business lasting this long, but because what were the odds that Jill would still be running it after all these years? And apart from all that, what the hell is his portrait doing in the window front and centre? Which is exactly what Granny Pamsy is trying to work out, scanning up at her husband's head, hair grey of course but still as thick and swept-back and the eyes still more than capable of hiding that almost-surfacing grin – so that Granny Pamsy and Granddad Jacko are both rendered momentarily motionless, not easy with three grandkids at hand – Abel reliving that last day after Jill had propositioned him, after they'd kissed goodbye, and reminded him (as though he could ever forget): *Think over my offer, half of everything, including me* – then out popped a camera for several snap-snaps of unprepared Abel, looking all the more surprised and open faced so that it would be plain easy for his grandson to recognise him a lifetime later … And as Abel relives those last parting moments, Pamsy can't help a few flashbacks to the Victorian power strike, the constant trips to Albury and … and … that one day when the roads were flooded … *They did some pressing for us during the power strike* … duh-uh … *remember I trucked the garments over here?* Double duh-uh … hardly a viable explanation for the presence of his in-your-face portrait in this window, so Abel makes a show of peering into the shop's glass casement, then straightens up and takes two kids' hands and marches on, away from another historic statement of his life framed and under glass, and Pamsy, after a moment's hesitation, finally breaks cover, *Always thought you fancied yourself a bit of a pinup boy,* and as Abel turns to decipher her meaning, Granny Pamsy overtakes him and walks ahead with third child, and Abel follows with face burning, for he glimpses a young Jill standing behind the counter, looking back at him, tight mouth chomping, exposed jade eyes and single gold earring transmitting that tantalising offer all over again, set of *Jacko* keys on the table, iridescent with a life of their own … *Jacko … can we have lunch there?* the oldest points at a fast food restaurant with pictures of superheroes adorning the walls, Captain *Shazam* Marvel amongst them. The five Marvins leave behind the boring dry-cleaning window and what-could-have-been … *Goodbye, Jacko,* the middle one sings out and soon the other two are giggling and joining in … *Goodbye, Jacko* they yell and wave … *Goodbye, Jacko* echoes in Abel's ears as he walks away from that shop window for the second time in his life until that morning two years later when the digital numbers descend to clutch his face in the pool and that damned white-clad nurse demands that before he can depart for anywhere he needs to stop to give a full account of himself.

Pamsy makes no secret of her admiration for her husband's effort, as the first Saturday of the month Abel gets up at five, packs a small plate of sweeties surrounded by ice, hugs and kisses his two boys and pregnant wife then drives the hours to Christmas Hills, where he spends the day and returns late at night … *You're a decent human being, Abel Jackson Marvin, to have such dedication to visit your sick friend. Give yourself a pat on the back, mate.*

His two boys aren't as enthusiastic about losing their daddy for the day but Abel consoles them thus: *Sometimes, some things in life can't be exactly how you want them to be.* Since Abel's return from his exodus in the warehouse, Pam has done her best to maintain an orderly household, and strangely enough, since Abel's monthly detours to The Shelter, loving words have crept back into her conversation. Her husband's concern for his friend seems to have melted the invisible wall between them, and after a long absence they are again touching in bed and Abel calls her *Pamsy* again while she revives plans to have a third child, *What do you say we try for that elusive daughter once more?* And Abel can hardly refuse that approach with his two youthful sister-squirrels so foremost in his mind and a daughter lovechild hiding in the bush and what-do-you-know in the blink of a CLANG DING WOOOP Pamsy is pregnant again, and what's more poignant in their reestablished relationship, they are going camping again, that pot-roast smell permeates the bush and Wags-Two goes ballistic chasing the kids between the trees … But all this is left behind as Abel drives down the slippery, steep hill, his excitement bubbles over, he shakes hands with the welcoming, walking forest – some walking strangely, some leering and slobbering, some saplings toppling, but all clapping and singing, *We shall overcome, in our deep hearts, we firmly believe, nature will see us through …* – then goes looking for Roma and his daughter; as the dining room comes into view, little Acacia charges breathless to *Dada Sweetie* and jumps into his arms as though propelled, and every month she's a little taller and a little heavier, sporting a wider grin; she snuggles into her father's arms, cooing like a pigeon, Abel carrying her up the hill; approaching Roma, the girl bounces up and down on his chest, giggling like crazy, intently watching her mother, waiting for that burst of crying laughter and she rises as high as possible and grasps them both into a group hug that she intends to hold forever ... *Dada Sweetie is here, Mama* ... while chanting, *Dada Sweetie, Dada Sweetie,* Acacia claws Abel's backpack until he digs up the sweetie plate with one lamington, one Chocolate Teddy, one Tim Tam and one meringue; *Easy does it,* Roma reminds her daughter, *just one little bit today, it's got to last a month* ..., Abel seeing Papaya gives her the ceramic white angel with the blue eyes and one stiff blue wing saying, *When you came to the pub that time I thought you were an angel. Take this good luck charm as a small token of my thanks.* Papaya, laughing, places the angel smack in the middle of the shelf in the centre of the dining room. Acacia jumps up for another hug to regain his attention ... The Shelter is all the life she's ever known; half-naked she tears through the trees and vegetable patches, laughing, playing, feeding the animals, digging in the sandpit, and helping with beading and basket-weaving, known as Cheeky but Abel soon starts calling her Cheek-Cheek ... *Here comes Cheek–Cheek and Dada Sweetie ... Must be first Saturday of the month again.* As his self-appointed guide, Cheek-Cheek drags Abel from one end of the farm to the other, chatting, introducing him to everyone, informing him of their work tasks and what problems they have, calling the sunflowers *Helianthus annuus* and the growing basil patches *Ocimum basilicum* ... After the first couple of visits Abel gives Roma a break by taking George with them, pushing the wheelchair up and down the hills, both Abel and Acacia chatting to George, sometimes Roma joins them, and they picnic under the elm trees at the end of the property ... Three people help look after George: Daffodil, a blonde buxom woman who can't stand to be indoors of any structure, even a car, sleeping on Roma's porch even during the coldest winter nights; Batman, a man Abel's age who's frightened of darkness, hence stays up all night and sleeps all day – he's George's night-nurse; Judge Nellie Tonne, an elderly fat lady who cries all the time and who's stark naked under her loosely hanging avocado sheet, an ex-family court judge whose 'normal' life ended when a disgruntled father who had lost a custody battle for his son killed her only son, blasting him with a sawn-off shotgun while they were having lunch, her clothes splashed head to toe with her son's blood ... *We look after damaged people* ... One day after the communal lunch Papaya negotiates with Acacia to borrow Abel and leads him down a narrow path through dense bush until they come to a cluster of elm trees at the far side of the property; crouching down low, they move duck-style towards the trees, Papaya holds a finger up to her lips, then gently parts the bushes before them. In the middle of a clearing sits a man under the shade of a colourful beach umbrella advertising a suntan lotion; he's wearing a black, three-piece pinstripe suit, heavy black glasses and his hair is parted and slicked back, a little like Clark Kent; a large brown-grey eagle is hunched rigidly on the grass opposite him, its feathers ruffled by the breeze, staring at the man with fierce yellow-black eyes while tinkling music plays in the background … *A wedge-tailed eagle*, Papaya whispers just as the music stops, the eagle rouses itself and flies up into one of the elms, contemplating the human below. The man stands up, dons sunglasses, as Papaya and Abel emerge from the shrubs – *Dr Joe Banana, I'd like you to meet Abel Marvin* – they shake hands, Papaya leaves, then the man unfolds another green chair and signals for Abel to sit – *I'm a communicator, Abel, the animals come to me with their problems, and believe me, I'm not short of clients –* he sighs – *mostly their problems are caused by humans.* Joe removes his sunnies, his eyes are older than the rest of his face, two withered triangles, tweaked to a point in the middle of the eyelids. He nods up at the eagle, *Lost his nesting site to a new sub-division. Lost his tribe and identity.* His black eyes roll restlessly like billiard balls … *I wanted to thank you, Abel, for coming here once a month. I know it's a hassle and a long drive, but you've done wonders for Roma and Acacia …* the billiard balls stop front and centre, waiting to be scattered: *You've anchored them, man, before you started coming here, they were floating without mooring* – *What about George?* – Joe shakes his head, *Keep doing what you're doing. Take George around, talk to him … severe haemorrhaging in the brain* – a hopeless shake of head – *you never know, miracles can happen, floods can subside, release can come in many forms …* the triangles contract in a grin, *I believe they call you Marvin-the-Magician, right?* Abel continues on with Acacia and George through the bush, his daughter points out the small gears on the side of George's wheelchair: *This one is for going uphill, this one for downhill, this one for idling …* Chatting away merrily, she points out trees and flowers with long, difficult, botanical names. Worn out from pushing the wheelchair, Abel falls asleep under a tree; on waking, his daughter is deeply engaged in a game with her dolly, plus at least half a dozen imaginary kids whom she loudly directs in a game; Abel watches with barely open eyes as she runs every idea past her tattered dolly – a local product that has spent most of its life half buried in the sandpit – the dolly's name is Child, and Acacia addresses her rather formally, *Would Child like a sweetie? … Would Child like to go for a walk with Dada Sweetie in the bush?* And throughout their walks, talks and laughter, George's flooded brain refuses to absorb any communication, not words, sounds, laughter, not one solenoid *DING* – if George can remain immune to Acacia's bursts of life, is there any hope of that flood receding? Saying goodbye to his daughter is excruciating: she cries, arms stretched out to him, *One more hug, Dada Sweetie … just one more hug … please* – does every solenoid in his playfield have to be charged with children clutching departing fathers' knees? Abel sobs for most of the long drive back home, and during the four weeks until the next visit he fills his vision with Cheek-Cheek's ringing laugh, and recalls her jokes and her made-up funny songs – *Baa, baa, white sheep, have you any milk?* – her terrible imitated bellbird call, and her favourite kookaburra laugh, *Ah-ah-ah-h-h-h-h-h-h* … His daughter – conceived by a mother with the taste of meringue on her lips – offers one to George from her carefully guarded cache – *Have a bite, George*, she moves it back and forth under his nose, but there's no response to the melting sweet flavour tingling his nostrils from arm's length. A mountain of sweeties …

Abel discovers with a bit of overland hiking he can save at least half an hour each way into and out of the farm, which means one more precious hour with his daughter, Roma and George. Abel begins using this back way, but still, some months later, when Pam is two weeks away from giving birth, the drive seems to take forever, stuck in peak morning traffic, all he sees through the windscreen is George's flooded mind, his body slumped to one side in the wheelchair, oblivious to the tantalising meringue under his nose. When he finally gets there Abel parks under a cluster of blue gums, tall and bushy with plenty of shade, and heads off on foot with his backpack into a scorching day, with a stifling north wind, and by the time he climbs up the back slope he's covered in sweat, blue bushflies stick to him like magnets, everything is dusty and dry and he can't remember the last time it rained ... But thoughts of all else take a hike as Papaya meets Abel outside the dining hall, points to Acacia who's sitting at the large wooden table drawing pictures with other kids. *Joe Banana asked if you could drop in for chat. This'd be a good time ...* her silent blue eyes – same as the ceramic angel's behind her – telegraph, *This isn't just a casual invite*, and although Abel is aching to hug his daughter, he tramples through the dry crackling leaves to Joe's 'consulting rooms'. *Ah, Abel*, Clark Kent points to a vacant canvas chair and Abel sits down. No eagle anywhere, Abel feels the emptiness inside the tinkling music ... *The most important part of being a communicator is to be a great listener. Silence speaks more than words. You've heard of Freud's talking cure, right? This is my listening cure* – head jerks up in mocking laugh

– *Listening gives the gears a chance to mesh in peace.* Abel could give Joe a run for his money as far as being a great, silent listener. He's had a lifetime of practice. He rewards Joe with a healthy dose of muteness and Joe attends … *I spend a great deal of time listening to George, and so does the eagle. George sits here, the eagle perches over there, and they listen to each other – man-made problems, Abel, all our own doing – but can we do something about it?* Two black eyes come to rest inside the withered triangles. Abel tells Joe all – without uttering a single word – *I killed a cat-killer – tossed him down the stairs. I betrayed a kind man, binge-fucking his wife.* Abel chuckles at the centred, black billiard balls: *I changed* MADE IN CHINA *for OZ labels, perved on hordes of naked young women, deserted my sisters …* The withered triangles crack into smiles and Joe speaks: *Had some sessions with Roma,* Joe nods, positive, *She feels that you, Abel and Acacia, are the only real parts in her life … what do you think of that?* Waves of silence flood out of Abel, and Joe nods, receiving. *Roma tells me that she equates life with the randomness of a pinball machine – how about that? – She'd spent her life trying to tilt the pinball machine …* Clark Kent throws his head back and laughs, *But you know what bothers me, Abel? That eagle you saw here – Mr Feathers – he really is powerless to alter his destiny – but you know, well, people, us, we do have choices right? … Stop, go, turn right or left, do this or that, we do have a little over that eagle, don't we? – You could have a point, Dr Joe –* Abel echoes in his head, *I'm still Abel and not Jackson, aren't I?* Joe studies his patient, absorbing Abel's comments. His face then scrunches up with weight and his hand shoots up to rest his chin: *Maybe if I listen to*

Roma long enough she'll work out how to lift that machine and alter some outcome, stop that Buckaroo horse bucking and kicking – She did, Abel replies in his head, *she draped us in capes and pulled me down on top of her and we made Acacia.* Joe nods, then Abel gets up – *Thanks for the chat,* Joe says.

Abel leaves the bush clearing, his mind already full of his daughter ... *Cheek-Cheek – Dada Sweetie ...* she flies into his arms, groping for his backpack, but Acacia knows the rules, some children are not allowed sweeties even once a month ... *Shhh* ... her little finger to her lips, she points at a large calendar, showing the crossed-out days since his last visit, and cuddles into Abel's neck, cooing like a pigeon ... *I love you so much, Dada Sweetie ...* Back down to earth, Abel waves to the white angel with blue eyes and single upright wing while Acacia drags her father to her mother's hut: *Dada, Dada ... Dada Sweetie is here, Mama ...* Roma stands, loose dress flowing, brushing streams of black silken hair, she stops and nestles into Abel's arms and Acacia does her favourite family cluster hug ... *Your daughter has prepared a one-girl show and an afternoon tea picnic in the bush, Dada ...* Roma's hands stroke Abel's trembling cheeks, *Dada Sweetie* loses consciousness for a few seconds, Roma has to repeat that sentence ... *High tea,* Acacia corrects her mother, shakes *Dada Sweetie* out of his reverie ... *Where's George? – Daffodil took him to Joe Banana's, he'll be back soon –* Acacia grabs dilapidated Child, pulls Abel's hand and leads them out the door, *Bye, Mama – Cheek-Cheek, haven't you forgotten something?* The little girl stops, furrows her brow, then breaks into a wide grin: *Just a minute, Dada,* she races back inside, seconds later comes back out in a pink tutu and beaming, *Aren't I beautiful, Dada?* She pirouettes then curtseys – it's Roma all over again, slipping into the pinnie basement in that other world – before ... *You are stunning, Cheek-Cheek – Let's go, Dada Sweetie – Not yet you don't, you need these,* Roma puts soft, white ballet slippers on her daughter's feet, *now you can do your show* – His daughter takes a few steps back, curtsies with self-conscious grin, clears her throat and begins singing Roma's pinball refrain: *Pull the pin, hear the ping* ... she doesn't just sing it, she acts it out, a fully-blown pantomime, leaning over the pretend pinball machine, head turned sideways in anticipation, pulling the pin, hand cupping ear to hear the ping, index finger waved in warning to *never, never, let the ball drain* ...

And it's all so worth it. So, so totally worth everything as Roma's black eyes flood with tears of enchantment, love thick and pliable and tangible and everything was so, so worth it ... *I'm finished, Dada Sweetie,* she brings Abel back to the present, *did you like it? ... we can go now* – Abel finds his voice: *Like this, in this heat and dust?* Acacia insists, so Roma shrugs as the little ballerina drags her father, Child and a picnic basket out the door ... *Bye, Dada Sweetie and Cheek-Cheek and Child,* Roma beams, waving bye-bye, *have a good time at high tea* ... Abel stops, rewinds, for sure it's the old Roma, the indispensible, essential Roma, the Roma from the pinball arcade, her face radiant; he walks back to give her a bear hug, she's airy, almost ethereal, and trembles in his arms ... camera at the ready ... *Sir Marvin-the-Magician ... look this way and smile* ... Mandrake cape tied on, Polaroid poised, *magic fingers spread ... hypnotise me, Sir Marvin ...*

click … photo out, paper stripped off, waves in the air … *Take care, my loves, the hot northern wind is blowing.* Roma kisses him, eyes glisten with happy tears, drawing out Abel's tranquil smile. *You bring us such joy, take care, my darlings.*

Old Abel shuts his eyes, locks his arms around his face but is unable to block out the vision of father and daughter walking past the cultivated fields and the strawberry hothouse, around the clearing where Joe Banana communicates with troubled animals and brain-flooded people, the consultation tingling with the heavy silence … Is that eagle sitting listening to George? Come next trip he'll bring the communicator a large plate of sweeties as thanks … for what? For listening. They can see Daffodil down the hill wheeling George back to Roma and they yell and wave frantically. The bush is arid and dusty and they look for shade and protection from the hot north wind that blows in their faces, the afternoon sky is a mess of black clouds, only rain can rebalance this nature … On top of a hill, under tall trees, Cheeky prepares their high tea; out of her wicker basket comes a set of red and white chequered mats, tiny plastic cups and saucers, plastic cutlery and rings through which she threads napkins, just like his early dinners at the McCullums', underplates and ceramic napkin rings; the little girl chatters to herself – flashback, *We're doing Virginia Woolf at school … Martha or Honey?* – she lays out her tea-set, measuring the exact distance between all utensils; once all is ready Cheeky peels the paper off the cupcakes, then claps her hands and announces they can now begin … Old Abel in the car, fighting for breath in the unbearable north wind, and young Abel cuddle his daughter, both Abels feel that danger creeping towards the top of that other, long-ago hill in the nature reserve, young Abel sitting on his bike, calling out to Wags, the thick north wind broadcasting an erratic Morse code of approaching danger; birds, the first to decode the signals, flap and squawk overhead; father and daughter have consumed their first two cupcakes when two cinders land on the picnic rug like advance scouts, a flaming kangaroo bounds through as though it's been bounding from fire since Abel was in knee pants, then a thundering – the world being savaged – catches up with its scouts, a helicopter buzzes overhead bellowing indistinguishable words, Abel sees a wall of black smoke and orange flames approaching, cannibalising the landscape, but he's no longer a boy sitting on his bike hypnotised by the fire front, as an adult he knows there's no chance of out-running it … the place thick with dry trees and bushes is paradise exposed … then he remembers … the creek below the hill, still deep even with no rain, Abel crossed it this morning; calmly he says, *Let's go do some water play, Cheek-Cheek*, and grabs the girl and the dolly and races down a dead-grass hill, the air so sparked with cinders and dust catching in their lungs … *We didn't pack up the picnic set, Dada – I know, Cheek-Cheek, I know – Hot, Dada* … Cheeky stretches her hand out to catch the black and red fireflies … They splash into the creek, embraced by its coolness, Abel sinks down to his knees in the mud holding his daughter, the fire front has reached the top of the hill, consuming their perfectly laid out picnic setting, but not enough of an offering, the crackling flames lean down the hill challenging the man and child in the water below – leering at the pathetic two crouching humans, cracking with exploding sparks – *This is water play, Cheeky, let's practise, I'll count to three, take a deep breath … like this, and we'll dunk under …* The flames race down the hill but there is precious little to ravage, there are no trees or bushes and the dry short grass is instantly consumed, transforming the brown earth to black and red, the smoke rolls in and their eyes start to burn … *One, two, three … big breath,* Abel covers the girl's mouth, and pulls her under water, when they resurface, she coughs and splutters and begins to cry, the heat has reached the creek's edge, scorching as an open furnace, the water begins to steam, Abel splashes the girl's head and shoulders … *One, two, three … big breath,* he forces his daughter under water again, Acacia, wild–eyed, struggles and kicks, but he forces them to stay under … The thick smoke presses down and when they emerge they gasp at what little air there is left above the water, hot cinders land around them like star showers, sizzling as they hit the water, Abel splashes warm waves like a windmill … *I want my Mama … I want my Mama – I know, sweetie, I know … not much longer, I promise …* Waves of smoky condensed hot air and whirling cinders press down … *Please, Cheek-Cheek … just once more … we have to – NO, DADA, NO …* Dunked twice more, the coughing girl is a limp wet rag in his arms … Abel looks around, *That's it, Cheek-Cheek, the fire is leaving, look …* He stands, hoisting her out of the water, with the air still a sauna, both cough, but watch as the main inferno engulfs the next hill towards The Shelter … but Abel can't think of that now, he splashes water onto the creek's bank and they crumple down onto the ashes, Abel is covered in mud, Acacia trembling and exhausted, a limp dripping doll of a muddy tutu-girl falls asleep in his arms, Abel kisses his daughter's tangled hair and murmurs a message to Roma, *I'm taking care, my love, your daughter is safe with me* ... When he regains his breath Abel carries sleeping Acacia over the hill, stumbling on the hot ground, and gasps at the sight: no more Shelter to be seen, the inferno has engulfed all, leaving only skeletons of smouldering trees, walls, sheds and chimneys, tractors like bombed-out tanks in a war zone, the charcoal stumps glowing red and black eyes like pulsating signposts to perdition ... Above, only the stillness of death, not a wing flapping, or a bill laughing, Joe Banana's clearing is all ashes – if any of his clients survive, their next sessions will cover serious issues ... No trace of the magical retreat of The Shelter he saw from the hill on that first day, no suggestion of blue shafts of light, blossoming trees, bright flower bushes, or avocado welcoming committee, the walking forest has been felled ... George's voice echoes inside his head: *Shangri-La, mate, the lost paradise.*

Abel's world begins to ebb, hugging his daughter to his chest, he collapses down on the black grass. As the smoke disperses like hell's curtain, a grotesque installation from the netherworld appears – the burned-out hulk of a white wheelchair, with a black corpse in it and another welded to the wheelchair, charred, red skeletons with gaping skulls and glaring eye sockets ... Cradling his daughter, Abel vomits, ice tremors race through his hot body, tears flood his eyes, he can't breathe; Judge Tonne, a black hippopotamus in avocado rags, struggles up to them, from being splashed with her son's lifeblood to being smeared with The Shelter's – Abel's trembling, wet eyes traverse from the burnt hulk to connect for the longest, most painful moment to the Judge's eyes – confirmation! ... She leans forward and gently kisses Acacia's sleeping head, then pushes Abel: *Go, take your daughter with you. Nothing here for you now, Abel.* A few others emerge from hiding places, like nuclear blast survivors, they stand, charred and stunned, unable to reconcile this new reality ... No time – Acacia murmurs in her sleep, Judge Tonne waves her arm, shooing him back. Unable to tear his eyes away, Abel consumes hell's sculpture; he turns – sleeping child in arms – and struggles up the hill, stumbling over unfathomable ground, his body broken parts, jigsaw pieces that no longer fit ... the uneven earth generates a hostile heat, his sneakers leave black rubber goo with each step, Abel's mind dips in and out of the past ... *Make love to me, Abel ... Give me the child we've been searching for – a baby to love and to hold or I'll die ... You bring us such joy, take care, my darlings* ... but she is dead now – dead – DEAD – a skeleton bonded to a wheelchair, but back, back, his mind falls, a live Roma drapes the cape over his naked shoulders, his head full of music, the scorched bush fills with Roma's perfume as she pulls him down, her tanned skin glowing in the overhead lights, her lips soft and warm, her lustrous hands stroke him into semi consciousness ... *You've saved Sir George-of-the-Jungle's life, Sir Marvin-the-Magician ... Please save Dame Gypsy-of-the-Romani* ... Afterwards, lying still, Roma stares at the ceiling … *Save Cheek-Cheek, Sir Marvin-the-Magician … She's all I've got … and all I'll ever have … You bring us such joy, take care, my love.* On top of the hill where they'd picnicked, a large black tree falls over with a thump that resonates tenfold within Abel, as like bedraggled pioneers they cross the river again, passing their wet, dunked impressions that will be there forever – then amazing, the rope ladder he'd climbed down that morning is intact, he wakes his daughter – *I'm thirsty, Dada – I know, Cheek-Cheek, I am too.* Abel places the girl on his back, and secures her with his belt … *We're going to climb up piggyback. Hang on as tight as you can.* Abel starts climbing, but the girl slumps, still sleepy, Abel comes down and switches her to the front … *This is much better, isn't it, Cheek-Cheek, I can see you now …* the sooty face breaks into a smile, her lovely black hair is tangled with ash … *We're going to Dada Sweetie's house, Cheek-Cheek … lots of sweeties there, we can be together every day …* By the time they reach the top Abel is covered in sweat and flies, he unstraps his daughter, wraps his arms around her like a tender bird and begins jogging – *I'm thirsty, Dada – Soon, Cheek-Cheek, soon, I promise –* running, stumbling and bumping it takes too long to reach the station wagon, he's never been happier to see it. He had imagined the bushy cluster of blue gums burned and collapsed on the car, but the trees are here, tall and intact, swaying their arrogance – no jet bumpers spewing fire on this playfield. He straps Acacia into the front seat and climbs in beside her. It's indeed a pleasure to be driving, Acacia is quiet, only occasionally murmuring that she's thirsty. Abel drives too fast, swerving and bumping over the rough unmade road ... *I'm going to spit out, Dada,* and she does, of course, car sick, regurgitated cupcakes everywhere, on her torn, muddy tutu. Abel pulls over, uses his shirt to clean his daughter and the car, gives her a big hug, *Dada Sweetie will look after you.* She snuggles into him, hooks a lethargic arm around his neck ... They stop in Yarra Glen; shirtless, black and dirty he carries the ragamuffin ballerina into the milk bar, and no one seems surprised; buys drinks and ice creams with soggy, mangled notes, and no one blinks. They sit on swings in the little playground under green trees that sway lethargically in the warm wind, all is peaceful and normal, kids climbing on the equipment, calling out and laughing – another world, a different playfield from the one he's just escaped ... Acacia sleeps most of the way home, but not peacefully, cries out, whimpers, clutches Child – now no more than a drowned rag doll – Abel rocks her gently with one hand, promising that all will be alright, tears trickling down his blackened face, the burned-out hulk of the wheelchair and two fused bodies wedged in his chest, *Roma ... Roma ... Roma* was one of them ... *ROMA! ... You bring us such joy, take care, my darlings ...* Too much time to think, maybe it's better to give in, drive fast, fall asleep, let the ball drain, drive over the cliffs where he'd rescued George and it'll all be over, let it finish where it started ... but Roma's last thought, as she was burning with unimaginable pain was that her daughter was safe with Abel ... *Make love to me, Abel ...* he can't stem the flow of tears, the most radiant personification of a woman ... so life-giving – so – so essential – and now ... ash. Abel makes it home, not sure if he's sane or crazy, desperate hugs from Pam – *I was worried sick, saw the bushfire on the news* – *My daughter, Cheek-Cheek, Acacia* – then he catches sight of the two of them in the hall mirror, the dirty urchin in a tutu and ballet slippers, clinging to the bare-chested chimneysweep; Abel cracks up, hysterical, he sees the scorched boy Abel staring into the fire truck's rear-view mirror. Pamsy stares open-mouthed … Acacia catches sight of Granny Annie's well-stocked tray on the table, big grin exposes white teeth in blackened face, *Dada Sweetie, I'm hungry* … Clutching lamington in one hand, choc-teddy in the other, the adults bathe the girl, and put her to bed, hastily washed and dried raggedy Child in one hand, Dada Sweetie's hand in the other, she won't let go until she's asleep; afterwards, in dressing gown, falling asleep while nursing tea, he tells his wife the full story of Roma … *After George was mangled at the protest … Roma found out that he could never … then one night in the pinnie basement* … by the time Abel finishes, he slumps on the table; without missing a beat Pam hugs her swollen tummy: *Looks like we have two new kids on the way* … Abel slowly gets up to embrace his wife with lead arms, but their brand new daughter cries out in panic, so Pam pulls a mattress into the room, and places it next to Acacia's bed; their two boys appear, silently watching – *Boys, meet your new sister, Acacia* – *Can we have a sweetie too?* – hands hugging stomach, Pam stands back and surveys the scene: *Better sleep here for a while, Dada Sweetie* … What did George ask him in the pub that winter's day? *Is she a good woman?* … Oh, George, George, George … look at her now, embracing someone

127

else's child without an angry word … the saxophonist flashes through Abel's mind, battling to fit a sudden new world into his established comfortable one – an image of George leaning forward drumming the dashboard flickers into life – *Who among us isn't an 'odd couple'?*

Abel removes the glass window slats and slips into the pinnie basement, the lights are ablaze, *Tommy* plays at full pelt. Abel nods at Roma's seven-year-old self, while Chief Frank with rolled up sleeves services the machines, *I used to do this on Sunday mornings, Roma in pyjamas* – he studies the framed picture – *brought breakfast down on a tray* – spruced-up Buckaroo, and Lucky Strike glow like the best silverware, playfields shiny as mirrors, Chief Frank wipes Paradise down with a soft cloth – *Roma'd help me, by the time she finished, food and tools littered the floor* – the basement smells of varnish, metho and machine oil, Chief Frank pulls the spring back and the metal ball launches like a rocket, he tests the flippers and they click with a life of their own, he wipes his eyes – *By the time she was three, we'd made up our own pinball chant, by fifteen she could beat me … a wizard … a 'she Tommy'* – he breathes long and hard – *the liveliest girl, couldn't sit still until she met George* – weak smile – *George stopped her in her tracks. 'I nearly lost him, Dad,' she said after you saved him, Abel, she fretted, she cried, then she'd smile, then 'Oh my God, I nearly lost George'* – Chief Frank shakes his head and wipes his eyes. Abel gets behind Buckaroo, looks at the playfield, the laughing horse just like Bernie. On the back glass the utopian image of the golden-haired girl hugging the golden horse's head, and below the mean Buckaroo, ready to buck and kick arse.

Abel grinds his sneakers into the cement floor, pulls back the plunger and launches a silver ball. CLANG – *Wags* – DING – *Dad* – WOOOP – *Mum* – WAAK – *Bernie* – OWOWOW – *Ginger* – CLANG – *Mary* – DING – *Granny Annie* – WOOOP – *Pamsy* – DING – *George* – WOOOP – *Roma* – DING – Jill – WAAK – *Papaya* – OWOWOW – *Acacia* – CLANG – *Joe* – DING – *Frank* … For the first time ever Abel says the names out loud … *The playfield is inclined upwards several degrees from where you're standing,* Chief Frank points out. He takes a silver ball and rolls it down the centre of the playfield glass, it falls off the cabinet's end and smacks on the floor at Abel's feet – *An uphill battle, even if you're an expert, the ball will keep coming back at you, forever* – Chief Frank picks up the ball and massages it in his fist: *You have no control over it, Abel, limited influence is your only tactic* – Abel wonders what Dr Joe would say in his bush consulting rooms. Would he bring up human choices again? Would his triangular eyes point out Jill's offer again? What would he make of Cheek-Cheek's new family? … The jet bumpers spring to light, the bells clang, the horse kicks and the man rotates. Well, Abel chuckles to himself, he did come here to exercise a small choice – *We're going to the playground in the park Sunday morning. Pam … Pam thought you might like to join us and play with your granddaughter* … Chief Frank steps forward and bumps into Paradise – is it possible that he's forgotten where the machines stand? – his body folds in half over it, the machine springs to life, a cacophony of numbers click over, bells ring, balls clanging and the hula girl on the back glass shakes her hips … Next

Sunday morning, Chief Frank cautiously walks to the swing set towards the Marvin family ... *Cheek-Cheek, say hi to your granddad* ... Acacia's face clouds over, of course Chief Frank had visited his granddaughter at the farm, but what other memories will this re-acquaintance drag to the foreground? ... *Mama has gone away for a while, you can stay with Dada Sweetie* ... Acacia began marking the days until her mother's return off the calendar ... *Granddad? ... Mama? ... Fire?* – both Abels pull back – *Pop?* the little girl twigs – *That's right ... hey, Acacia, did you know that when I was little like you, my granddad, also Pop, used to try and catch me on the swing?* ... Abel starts pushing from behind, but the girl isn't pumping her legs, face still clouded, a memory lurks on the verge, Pop makes a feeble grab, then collapses on the grass ... *I nearly caught you, Cheek-Cheek* ... the girl's face cracks into a grin, Pop does it again, letting the girl's legs slip through his arms, he complains bitterly, clowns, falls, and Acacia bursts into raptures ... Sometimes, when sitting at the kitchen table, Acacia gets a longing, faraway look staring at the large paper calendar on the opposite wall, those numbers and squares used to mean something important, but she can't quite lock onto what. Occasionally, after a long calendar stare she'll cry out at night, whimpering *Mama, Mama* ... in her sleep, and Abel, who's slept with one ear open since he brought her home, jumps up and calms the girl down with gentle rocking, *It's okay, Cheek-Cheek, everything is fine, Dada is here.* Pamsy by then has already pulled out the spare mattress and Abel lies holding his daughter's hand until she's calm. His family are used to waking in the morning to see Daddy sleeping on the floor next to her bed. Pop is good therapy for Acacia, she smiles whenever he comes into view, a kind of bridge from the old to the new, so the Marvins make sure that they see the old guy as often as possible. But how can Chief Frank be *Pop* to one Marvin child, and leave the other three behind? Not possible! Next Sunday lunch at the Marvins' … *I'm Pop, your grandfather* … the two older boys unwrap their presents and it's not until later in the week that the question arises, *Whose daddy is Pop?* Abel simply substitutes Chief Frank for a pseudo father … 'Odd couple' indeed! Odd family! The 5×M+D concept fades further into oblivion … Pop often invites the Marvins for Sunday brunch, including the McCullums; Abel, sitting back surveying this happy, raucous scene, is filled with uncontrollable sorrow: why can't Roma and George also be there? Naturally the pinnie basement becomes the king attraction, the kids, standing on boxes, are soon taught how to play the ancient machines, and they shriek with delight singing Roma's pinball mantra over and over. Abel watches the silver ball ricochet from bumper to bumper, he balls his fists over his missing best friends and kicks the machine leg tilting the playfield. *Did I have a choice?* Abel ponders – *I could've, should've been at George's side, pulled him away from the horse* – the white-clad nurse hovers over his shoulder just to remind him: *Have you given a full account of yourself, Abel?* – Pop supervises the squealing and the balls shooting all over the place; Pamsy says: *Got yourself an instant family, Pop, didn't even need to add water.* In desperation to keep Roma close Abel hires the DVD of *Who's Afraid of Virginia Woolf?*, sits down with Pamsy to watch it, explaining about the long-ago banter at the McCullums' dinner. *Honey ... Honey,* Abel mutters and sees nothing of the explosive play except for that one role: *Can you believe that Roma played this scatterbrained woman?* Pamsy has only met Roma twice, at both weddings; before that she'd constructed an abstract image of this *wonder woman.* An impression only enhanced at the young McCullums' wedding, when the jolly, slightly drunk groom – in white suit and shirt with white gardenias pinned to his white cravat – stood up and announced with rolling ebullience: *How lucky am I to be marrying this Romani princess? Did you know, ladies and gentlemen, are you cognisant of the fact that the Romani people left India one thousand years ago and they BUCKED, CLANGED and PINGED through Asia and Europe for a millennium just to bring this amazing woman here today?* Pamsy well understood what he meant, princess indeed, tall suntanned Roma, onyx eyes, coiled jet-black plaits spliced with gardenia rings, white lace wedding cloak with hood and Pam's husband with stars in his eyes, transfixed by that image but no more than Abel now, watching the DVD, with open mouth as the story rolls out to the child that never was, and childless Honey suddenly yells and cries: *I want a child ... I want a baby ...* the gap clamps shut between the actress and Roma; Honey is Roma and Roma is Honey; had Roma ever thought back on that role and wondered if it was just another quirky bounce of that silver ball being cast in the play as that barren woman? When Chief Frank passes away, he leaves his big house to the Marvins. They lease the place, sell the machines but keep Roma's three favourite pinnies, Buckaroo, Lucky Strike and Paradise. Abel can't pin down when or how it starts, but teen Acacia, as she shoots the balls to their sizzling lit-up targets, mechanically sings along: *Pull the pin, hear the ping* … but then a sense of foreboding closes in on Abel, he sees little Acacia sitting on the swing that first day Pop came to the park, the clouds crossing her face … And that damned ghostly nuisance of a nurse suddenly discards her foggy shroud and faces up front and centre in the middle of the windscreen and finally it's Nurse Peggy, looking him straight in the eye.

For a couple of years the warehouse hires Nurse Peggy as its first-aid officer, and as she finally faces off Abel the foggy steam in the car dissipates, Nurse Peggy calls his name and asks him, as she did back then, *Have you given a full account of yourself, Abel?* … From the first day she joins Product Line they have a natural connection as Nurse Peggy is the only other non-Vietnamese employee. Peggy, white starched uniform including small upturned bonnet, spends her lunch breaks talking to Abel having a coffee and sandwich in his assistant manager's cubicle, and while he's munching away she tells him of her years as a palliative nurse. Sometimes, as she scans the steel beams of the warehouse roof, it seems she's telling herself the story of her own life, or perhaps re-dreaming it, and Abel practises the Dr Joe-taught therapy of solid, silent listening … *The patients in my charge were already dead, it was just a matter of keeping them in the best possible order until their clocks ticked down and ran out* – old Abel stiffens, his own pool clock epiphany rings in his ears – *Of course*, Peggy states, her body coiled around the recollection,

I greeted them with my most sparkling eyes and cheeriest words – hello, welcome, nice to have you with us – faking, of course, that everything we did, the post-treatments, killer-drugs and placebos, had a promised future – whether to cure, or muzzle the hungry beasts gnawing away at their brains, hearts or lungs or blood or ovaries and so on … I was a conjurer of hope where there was none, and so they believed in me as a last resort – what choice did they have? Peggy watches a passing parade of ghosts on the warehouse ceiling: *Short fairy tales of hope, and they soon saw through the smoke and mirrors of course, and had to confront what was lurking on the other side … a black nothing … the only real hope was the blessing of a painless passage. They talked to me – a lot. I mean, what else did they have?* Peggy pours another coffee, patting down her multiple pockets, maybe searching for a lost face along the way: *Talking was perhaps – and definitely so in the end – the best medicine, the only medicine – recalling their lives, getting some closure, speaking softly for hours on end, as though I was keeping a ledger, and would present it back to them before their last breath was gasped so they could sign off … hah!* – a short hard laugh escapes her mouth – *never happened quite like that, though …* Peggy thinks it over, then: *Most – well, all – had regrets … I should've done this, and that, I shouldn't have done this or that, I should've married him not him, her not her, shouldn't have had kids, had more kids, should've taken off in a caravan and got lost, shouldn't have been in denial … One guy, in pain – massive pain, no matter what we gave him, writhing in it – said he had no regrets except one giant one, and it filled him with such rage that his face became even more balloon-like than all the cortisone, chemo and other fucking shit-load of drugs combined* – Peggy cups her mouth – *'scuse the French. When he was a youngster he wanted to impress girls so he bought an old 1957 Jaguar, a big green car, but a piece of junk, metal bits fell out when he changed gear*s – Peggy laughs, at ease, her eyes sparkle – *When he couldn't stand the car any longer he traded it in, but then discovered that the used car dealer had dudded him, it was a 1954 model, not 1957, worth practically nothing; this old chap, literally on his deathbed, said he'd never forgive himself, how could he have been so stupid so as not to check the engine number of the car – felt that he'd given a full account of himself and could die happily if 'I could first choke that fucking used car salesman.' – You know what I told him, Abel? I told him he was a lucky man if that was his only regret* – Peggy shakes her head – *'I should never have bought that car,' he kept repeating – it was the last thing he said when he gave up his ghost.* Peggy sighs: *This is just one anecdote of dozens …* She drains her coffee: *One woman I looked after, with no hands and forearms – you know what she said before dying? – 'I never complained about drinking from a water bottle stuck in my armpit, never asked "Why me?", why my life was outside of normal life; all I wanted to do – all I dreamt about – was to have just one decent arm wrestle'* – Peggy laughs – *She'd seen this movie about some renegade women who went around the country hustling men, they'd challenge them to arm-wrestling comps, beat them and scoop up the money … she said: 'I could give a full account of myself if I could just once wrestle a man's arm flat down to the table with a bang.'* Lunchtime over, Peggy gets up to do her rounds, she takes off her bonnet, pats down her curls of short blonde hair in the small wall mirror, then fastens the starched white cap back into place. *They all had stories,*

Abel – she tells the mirror – *never-ending stories, but the one conundrum that bothered most people before they died – men and women alike, rich or poor – was: have I given a full account of myself? – Did you ever offer a plate of sweeties to balance out the nasties of life?* Abel tells Peggy about Granny Annie, and she laughs at her image, dabbing away smiling tears, *What a sterling idea ...* Little Acacia takes flight on the swing set, squealing with delight as she kicks and refolds her little legs. Abel catches the girl in mid-swing, *Acacia, meet your granddad, Pop ...* Acacia's face clouds over, buried trauma fights to resurface, *Mama gone away ... Mama ... George ... fire ... hot ...* Nurse Peggy turns her soft blue eyes back onto Abel and silently states: *That's what it comes down to in the end, matey, giving a full account of yourself.*

The memory of Nurse Peggy calms Abel, dampening the anxiety waves that swamp him in the pool ... *Have you given a full account of yourself, Abel?* In all of his actions, since building the wood-block city under Wags's watchful eye, did he do the best he could? *Well, didn't I? ... Nothing left undone? ...* Nurse Peggy's ghost points at the ticking clock above the pool: *It's an asset, not a threat. Every fragment of time points to the pleasures that life kicks up in its wake ... So what if occasionally he bought an old car without checking the registration plates? Swallowing the mistakes, he'd absorbed and digested them, and shitted them out long ago.* Nurse Peggy confirms: *You conjured up hope for George and Roma, and poor Roma, you gave her the one thing she thought was beyond her ... You helped Roma sit down at the table for that one, elusive arm wrestle ... In those last horrible minutes of that burning hell, Roma knew you'd* saved her daughter ... *You gave that white angel to Papaya that saved her life, didn't you? Jill's offer for the new Jack & Jill, that took some turning down, Jacko. – More to it than that, Nurse Peggy,* Abel points out, *If you save someone's life, are you responsible for them forever?* Short, sturdy Nurse Peggy in her ghostly, white uniform explains to Abel that he has no other options but to answer it himself and live with the bottom line. *I should've, I could've, then George'd be alive today, campaigning about this or that and* Honey *would be hugging her kids* ... Yes, Abel is free, but why still so restless, why so preoccupied with that dammed digital clock? He has his Pamsy, his four kids and seven grandkids, and for sure, he'll miss the *thanks, mate, thanks, dearie* at Welfare House ... And yet that irritating apparition won't leave him alone – what has he left undone? The pressure in his chest, the burned-out hulk of the wheelchair and two gaping skeletons, Acacia on the verge of memories on the swing in the park ... no, he has not yet given a full account of himself ... what has he left yet to do? Abel relaxes into a sleepy stupor, ignoring the pressure on his arms, the itchiness – if he could just – let go, close his eyes, let the ball drain, *Sir Marvin-the-Magician, hypnotise yourself, Abel, just let go ... Listen to Chief Frank, that ball will never stop rolling at you. You need to let that ball drain* ... But he isn't done yet, he needs to grab hold of the excitement machine's steering wheel and guide it out of this steaming fog menace ... Acacia's face clouds over ... the name-calling hushes to a whisper, several whispers ... *Go on, Sir Marvin-the-Magician, go for it – you're not done yet ... the road to this Ithaca is straight and clear, no Cyclops, Poseidon and giant cannibals to harass you on this journey* ... One eye opens, closes, then opens again, white steam inside the plastic dome, condensation covers the oxygen mask, hard to move, the room buzzes, both eyes open now, a mask over his mouth and nose, but only a little steam, the white-washed room is packed, four children with partners and seven grandkids crowd his bed, all holding paper plates with one sweetie in each ... *Jacko ... sweeties ...* The oxygen mask is lifted off, the corner of a lamington is pressed against his dry lips then whisked away, Pamsy stands next to his pillow, squeezing his hand, smoothing his hair back, the grandkid hordes press closer with their sweetie plates, Tim Tams, choc-teddies and meringues, white and pink ... *Roma's crumbs on the vodka bottle neck ...* Abel whispers to Pamsy, *I'm here, I made it ...* his voice is weak, Abel struggles to lift himself off the pillow, grimacing with pain – *Abel, what are you doing ... lie down – I'm giving myself a pat on the back, luv ...*

On his first day back at the pool Abel walks out of the changing rooms to the edge of the water, and a crowd mobs him. At The Shelter the green walking forest greeted him, now it's the wet fish brigade – the barrel-chested man, the woman in the glistening black and white striped bathers, even the two breast-stroking women, the lifesaving unit – rush up to Abel prepared to slap his back but are somewhat restrained by the healed bypass surgery scars on his chest, so they gently tap his arm: *We'd have rolled out the red carpet if we knew you were coming, Abel – so good to have you back, take it easy, ha ...* Not even one *have you given a full account of yourself, Abel?* ... When the crowd disperses, Abel's eyes drift up to scan that mongrel clock, digital numbers ticking away, folding into themselves, but just a bloody clock, nothing sinister this time; still Abel is reluctant to take chances, *Look, I understand*, he tells the clock as he slowly commences lap one, *Leave me be. I'm on it …* As he swims the abstraction of the burned-out wheelchair still rattles in his chest and Abel knows it is time to put it to rest. When Abel finishes, he gets out of the pool, and the staff have rolled out a red towel for him to step on, Abel breathes in and out deeply, and look, no steam, still smiling he meets his daughter in the foyer, *Here I am Dad, Mum's looking after the kids, got the day off and a tank full of petrol, now, what's the big mystery?* Acacia drives her father to Granny Annie's house, casting silent glances at him, she knows there's no use hurrying the process … Once they're at home Abel takes Acacia into the bedroom, opens the cupboard and takes out a large, flat white carton, which he puts on the bed. Abel's hands shake: *There are things you need to know, Cheek-Cheek, I should've told you before … but these things aren't easy … Acacia, luv, I need to tell you that your mother isn't your mother … Pam isn't your mother … your mother was called Roma, she died in a bushfire when you were a tiny tot –* Acacia sits, immobile – *I need to tell you this truth, Acacia, I owe it to your mother … I need to reunite the two of you …* Abel opens the carton, on top is a large envelope that he turns over and photos fall out, *The Knights and Dame of the Pinnie Basement Gang … Sir George-of-the-Jungle … Sir Marvin-the-Magician … And your mother, the magnificent Dame Gypsy-of-the-Romani …* Acacia turns pale, with shaking hands she lifts the set of faded

Polaroids, one by one, holding them up to the light; in tears, she turns to her dad, then back to the photos, she closely examines her mother's shiny eyes and bursting smile … *My mother?* She lifts the picture and slowly kisses it. She does the same to Roma's seven-year-old pinball photo, kissing the glass. Out of the box come the three capes, groaning with stiff joints as they're unfolded; Abel drapes the magic cape over his shoulders, spreads George's on the bed, drapes the Romani flag on Acacia's shoulders, then pops the dusty red jockey hat on her head, and they stand, looking in the bedroom mirror, Abel strikes the Mandrake pose, right hand outstretched, hypnotising, they both laugh but their eyes brim with tears … Abel takes a photo of his daughter and cape on his phone, compares it to Roma's, then sends it off … *Mum is waiting for this …* Their eyes lock on the word *Mum*, as though it's floating with tiny wings in the air between them … Then framed-under-glass rescue article and Bravery Award, then George's article on The Shelter, then the Melbourne demo and George's accident, then the bushfire reports and photos, too graphic, Acacia looks away, *I used to have flashes in my sleep … tall woman with coils of black hair … me naked in a sandpit … a bulky metal wheelchair grating on a gravel path …* Abel hugs his daughter and she continues, sobbing, *Sometimes, nightmares … fires, and splashing water … I thought they were remnants of childhood stories or maybe books – Pop was your grandfather, Roma's dad, you were the only family he had left …* The old, yellowing articles unfold with arthritis, they read together … *Children of Peace Christmas Hills fire, twelve dead …* in the bottom of the box, the pink tutu and white slippers, Abel chuckles, *Mum … Mum washed these several times, bleached and starched them … She said … she said that it was like the stork had brought you to us, a little bitty chimneysweep in black tutu … Child, your favourite dolly, a little worse for wear* – Acacia grabs the rag doll and hugs her. The picture of George falling backward at the demo, *George doesn't recognise me, doesn't know who I am,* back to Roma in Romani cape grinning … *Your mother was the most amazing woman … so striking, I couldn't look at her for too long … when your mother touched people, she … she became less – had to – gave a little bit of herself …* Abel picks up the ceramic angel with the blue eyes, the one stiff blue wing still intact – *Papaya sent it back to me after the fire. Said it had brought them luck, they hid in the cellar beneath the shelf it stood on …* Still wearing the jockey hat Acacia drives her father to Christmas Hills, Abel tells his daughter his life's story, from the day he lost Wags in that first bushfire, to walking in on his mother and Bernie, to the two couples splitting up and remarrying, to being chucked out of home to live with Granny Annie, *I was so lonely, Cheek-Cheek, but after I met George and your mother, I lived part of my life in a parallel universe …* They stop on top of the hill before driving down, it's drizzling, Abel waves his hand describing the splendour of the Biblical blue sunbeams streaming down that first day – the mirage of Shangri-La – Acacia wonders if the lily is being gilded, but is thankful the memory isn't of the monstrous fire of that last day; today trees and flowers are shrouded in mist, people work peacefully in the fields, no trace of that long-ago inferno … *'Shangri-La, mate, the lost paradise,'* George *called it … not bad, ha?…* They drive down, The Shelter is now Echo Farm, no signs of *damaged people,* Abel walks Acacia through her mother's history, the dining hall now a barn, the rebuilt hut they'd lived in, the gravel path with the grotesque installation art – Acacia grips her father's arm – then to Joe Banana's ex-consulting room, just a bush clearing now, no eagles or George or Roma – *he listened, he just listened to people in silence* – then to the top of the hill, the elm trees rejuvenated … *This is where you set up high tea – red and white chequered napkins, red tea cups and plates – I dreamt about them,* Acacia blurts out, still the same little Cheek-Cheek … Down to the creek: *This is where, about here …* Acacia wades in, stands in knee-deep water, tears roll down her cheeks as she watches her father on the grassy bank … On their drive home – in the front seat grown Acacia in wet jeans not so different than young Acacia on that other horrendous drive – the pressure is starting to ease in Abel's chest, the burned-out hulk of the wheelchair, Roma and George's gaping skeletons, are still there, and probably always will be, but they seem to have found their own angle of repose, they shift with his body's rhythm, integrate into it … Pam is waiting at Granny Annie's house with two colourful paper plates full of sweeties, covered with Glad Wrap; she hands them over and Acacia asks, *Where now? – You'll see.* They drive to the cemetery, strip off the cover and place the two plates beneath Roma and George's headstones. *My Granny Annie said: 'A plate of sweeties to balance out the nasties of life'* … Acacia stands, stooped at her mother's grave … *Your mother was such an astonishing woman; I sometimes doubted she was real,* Abel laughs, *thought I'd conjured her up … a fantasy … a wish … But it doesn't end here, Cheek-Cheek …* Back at Granny Annie's house, in the glassed-in patio, his daughter runs to the side cabinet and flings open the doors, stacks of old comic books fill the space, Abel takes out the old MAD magazine, blows off the dust – *What, me worry?* he says – Acacia looks at her father – *George worried about the world … that's why your mother loved him so much –* Abel switches on the three pinball machines: *Your mum was a pinnie wizard, could beat anyone … this was her favourite …* Acacia drapes the Romani cape over her shoulders, goes to Buckaroo, and grinds her sneakers into the wooden floor, flexes her shoulders, pushes the red hat backwards and winks at her father. She pulls back the pin, shoots out the metal ball, tests the flippers and softly croons: *Pull the pin, hear the ping, silver ball bounce and ding …* It's little Acacia in The Shelter all over again, performing her pantomime, singing and rotating arms with a mesmerising ballerina's grace. Roma's ghost lifts her lustrous hands off the flippers, swivels them in the air and, smiling at Abel, allows the ball to drain … *You bring us such joy, take care, my darlings …*

ACKNOWLEDGEMENTS

This novel's cacophony of pings and dings would never have made it onto the pinnie playfield had it not been for a few tilts of the machine by some strong literary minds. Thanks to Lauretta my 'in-house' structural engineer for the initial slants and tips. Thanks to Ada Moshinsky QC, my first stop outside muse for massaging a few spins and thwacks. Thanks to Linda Nix of Lacuna who locked into the *Sweeties* vision and scooped up the ball before it drained.

The biggest thanks to Jessica Perini. My silver ball surely bounced off the right jet bumper when I picked Jessica as my editor. Jess has the skills and passion. She cares.

ABOUT THE AUTHOR

Leon Silver has lived a life which is varied and full of travel. He was born in Shanghai, grew up in Israel, and came to Melbourne in the mid 1950s, where he still lives with his wife Lauretta. With a strong education in textile technology and design, Leon worked in the fashion industry for many years, but he has been writing all his life. After the publication of *Dancing with the Hurricane* (HarperCollins, 2004), and with five more novels in his top drawer, Leon ceased work to pursue his passion and brave it as a full-time writer.

Leon Silver
Photograph by Sid Buchbinder

www.ingramcontent.com/pod-product-compliance
Ingram Content Group Australia Pty Ltd
76 Discovery Rd, Dandenong South VIC 3175, AU
AUHW010727280225
407672AU00001B/1